Return
of the Black Knight

OMAHA, NEBRASKA

RETURN OF THE BLACK KNIGHT

Author Photo by Ruth Ploof

Cover Photo by Tahoe
Cover and Interior Design by Maple Cat Design
Manuscript Edited by Matt Case

ISBN-13 978-1973568605

*Dedicated to Samuel Thomsen,
a great friend
who was like a brother.
May Elohim wrap you in His wings.*

The Family of the Moon

Beta: Captain Cody
Winter Wolf: Anna
Wolf Princess: Katie
Wind Wolf: Hailey
Storm Wolf: Ash
Moon Wolf: Ezeryah
Time Wolf: Jenna
Sun Wolf: Alezandra
River Wolf: Heather

Army of the Moon Leaders

Beta Moon: Captain Cody
NightWolf: Captain Delthar
NightFang: Captain Edward
NightGuard: Captain Zander
NightHunter: Captain Matthias
NightBlade: Captain Samuel

"Live a life that is meant to be lived, Feel what is meant to be felt, Draw the sword that is meant to be drawn, Fight the fight that is meant to be fought, Love who is meant to be loved, Forgive who is meant to be forgiven, Save the life that is meant to be saved, Lead that which is meant to be led, Fear only what is meant to be feared, all in the name of Elohim and His Son, Emmanuel"

-Alpha Commander Wolf

When there were knights who battled a fierce enemy bent on controlling the world. This story is that of a young girl, a dream, and a mission. It's my story. A tale of brave warriors. And the possible return of a demon long dead.

-Ezeryah, the Moon Wolf

Now, faith is the substance
of things hoped for,
the evidence of things not
seen.

~Hebrews 11:1

Chapter 1

Ghost out of the Shadows

My breath was like frost as I gazed about a forest that was covered in snow, feeling a harsh wind blow about me. My skin stung from the icy cold. Giant snowflakes fell to the ground around thick pines. I appeared to be alone on a path that cut through the trees. Where was I, WinterFang Forest? Was this all real? Or could I be dreaming? Snow crunched under my feet while I walked, slipping on the uneven ground. Regaining my balance, I continued on through the frozen wonderland. The ice like air made it hard for me to breathe as the wind tried to steal my breath.

I heard footsteps behind me, thankful to have my sword at my side. Spinning around I saw my younger sister running toward me. She wore her brown robe which flowed with the wind as she ran.

"Ezeryah!" she called out. "My dear sister at last I found you."

"Jenna? What's wrong?"

I could tell my sister had been running a long distance, for she often found it hard to breathe.

"Demons are coming!"

My eyes grew wide, "What?!" I cried. "When?"

"I don't know."

"Does Father know?"

"No, I came to find you first."

"Quickly, we must warn him."

But as we started down the path, I heard a faint growl and a hiss.

"Jenna, did you hear that?"

She did not answer. Standing still I saw shadows of the trees form on the ground. They seemed to reach out at me, as if closing in for the kill. My legs trembled with fear. I turned to Jenna who was stopped in mid step. I put my hand on her shoulder and realized she was frozen, her eyes still as stone. As I thought of what to do next, a scent turned me towards the path that seemed to go deeper into the forest. Smoke appeared around the trees as I saw fire in the branches. The snowflakes ceased as all became night and the snow on the ground vanished.

The heat of the fire caused my eyes to fill with tears. A hot dry wind arose causing the branches of the trees to dry and crack.

It was then that I heard a deep growly voice like a ghostly whisper, "Ezeryah."

My heart stopped for a second. Who here besides my sister knew my name? The voice seemed to come from all around me, like a deadly whisper. As the sky turned almost pitch black, a figure of smoke appeared from the trees like a ghost out of the shadows. The flames seemed to follow it while it walked towards me. As I watched, an army appeared behind the smoking form who was much taller. Each one had black flames coming from the armor. Then I saw the glowing red eyes like fire as black armor appeared on the tall figure.

It couldn't be, could it? There was a look in the knight's fiery eyes, a dark and fierce desire. I tried to draw my sword but it was gone. The shadowy character was coming closer with each passing second while drawing a grizzly black sword. Fear crept up my arms and back to my neck. I was backed against a tree.

My heart beat like a butterfly's wings and I could feel the blood within both legs race like lightning, causing my knees to tremble. I felt weak as my legs would not move. As if my entire body was frozen with fear.

I was alone again, death was coming.

Chapter 2

Voldar's Reeth is coming!

I awoke in my bedroom lying on my back, staring at the ceiling. I looked at the clock on a nearby wooden desk, 6 a.m. Sweat flowed down my face like a flood. I turned to Jenna as she slept in her bed.

What was this dream? Armored knights led by... I tried to shake the image from my head. My heart was pounding so fast, it could have leapt from my chest. I was too scared to go back to bed. It seemed like the same haunting dream from the past several nights. But this one was different. Every dream before it had been in different places. There was a desert, a castle, a cliff, and several others.

Had this actually been a dream? Did I really see who I thought I saw? Getting down on the floor, I pulled out a box from under the bed, opening it to find the Moon Sword. The beautiful dark blue blade had three moons inlaid within each side. A smile spread on my face to find it still there. I stood up and walked to my window, it was snowing.

I thought to myself, "It's already December, snow has come at last."

The year was 2357. Snowflakes floated down through the air to the ground making the landscape look like a winter paradise in Southern Ireland. This is my favorite time of year, mostly because Voldar's Reeth was fast approaching. Voldar's Reeth means Zion's Peace. It is a week of celebrating Elohim and His Son, King Emmanuel. From December 15th to December 22nd presents exchanged. A candle is placed in a window each day until there are a total of seven in the house. On the twenty third day an eighth candle is placed in the center of the house. This candle is usually larger as it represents the war that we fight.

I turned and sat on my bed near the window staring off into space. I am known as the Moon Wolf because like the rest of my family members, I have the ability to transform into a wolf. Every full moon the strength of my wolf form is enhanced. I am also one fourth angel. I am thirty-nine years old, although in human form, I still look twenty. I can't explain it. It is said that when one reaches the age of twenty, that soldier's life is extended, but his or her body features always look the same.

Standing and walking to the window, looking out over fields and forests outside, I saw great shadows revealed by the light of a silver moon. The moon was oddly high for this time of night.

I knew my other sisters, Katie and Hailey would be on their WolfDragons, as they were every morning. I admit, my family is rather unusual. I suppose I should get into a bit of that.

I am the daughter of a knight named Captain Cody. He is the Beta Captain of my Grandfather's army. He is also the main leader of a group of men called the Army of the Moon. They are warriors, fierce warriors who fight with double bladed swords. My father came many years ago to Ireland to find these men. While here he met my mother, Anna, and they fell in love. Over the years, the force known as the Army of the Moon, welcomed several different types of soldiers, men from around the world.

There were the NightWolves of course. Then came NightFangs, ferocious archers who rarely missed their target. They wore their assyrian bows around their backs. They get their name from the fang tips on their arrows. Then came NightGuards, who were bigger, and stronger than most, and fought with giant zweihander swords which were strapped to their backs.

A few years after that father trained soldiers to become NightHunters. They were good at tracking and hunting, and could move with great speed, like a snow hare. Poniard daggers were their primary weapons. NightBlades came after that. They were quicker than most with a sword, using mostly rapiers. All of the Moon Soldiers are knights, but in a sense, they are also all ninja like, silent and deadly.

I picked up a pencil and notebook from my desk and sat on the bed. I loved to write and had been waiting for an idea for many months, but to no avail.

My Grandfather always said, "When you write, write about the things you love."

The problem was there were too many things that I loved. A few years back I wrote a short story about a girl who found a talking wolf. My family loved it, but I wanted to write something bigger. The white walls and ceiling of my room were offering no hope for my imagination. I looked at a picture of my family on my dresser. There were nine of us. Each of my siblings and I wore certain colored robes and armor pertaining to our wolf forms. As the Moon Wolf, I wear grey robes.

I looked to my sister Jenna still sleeping. She had the power of time for she was called the Time Wolf. Her brown robes hung near the door to our room. She could stop time, rewind, or fast forward it. She could also travel through time to different moments in history. I remembered a few months ago when she took me on a journey to 1776, six hundred years earlier, to witness the signing of the Declaration of Independence for the country of America.

Brushing my long brown hair from my face, as I turned back to my window, I sensed the wondrous aroma of breakfast downstairs. Glancing at the clock on the dresser, I was stunned to see 8 a.m.! Had I been sitting here for so long daydreaming?

Deciding to see how the holiday decorating was going I left the pencil and notebook on my bed. I walked into the long hallway down the wooden stairs I saw another of my sisters, Alezandra. She sat on the floor in what we called the Middle Room untangling lights for the tree. She had long black hair and wore bright yellow robes with a hood.

My mother and older brother were putting up the tree in a corner of the room between two couches. It was a tree they had cut down that very morning. My brother was dressed in a blue shirt with the face of a black wolf. Usually he wore blue and black armor with a black cape. He is the Storm Wolf. The pleasant sound of "Joy to the World" flowed from speakers in the house. The walls of the room were made of cedar wood reaching a height of twenty feet. On the West side of the room was a fireplace. An oak table was in the middle of the room while three couches were set in a square shape around it.

"The tree looks beautiful, Ash."

My brother turned to me and smiled, "It will look even better with the lights on it. We were lucky to get it in here."

"How tall is it?"

"Twelve feet."

"That must have taken awhile to cut down."

Ash nodded, "Father helped."

"Yea, that would do it."

I saw the silver star for the treetop on the couch behind me, "Ash, thank you for being here for Voldar's Reeth."

My brother turned to me. Looking at the snow outside he replied, "Africa is a long way off. While sand is nice, I wouldn't miss this type of sand for the world."

"Yeah, snow is better than sand."

Ash almost fell over from laughter, "Good one. Cold sand, hot sand, same thing to me."

"Yeah, snow is just cold sand."

Our mother moved around from the other side of the tree, dressed in her usual white robes, as she methodically straightened the twigs of the branches.

"And how are you?" she asked.

"Could be better," I replied.

"How so?"

"I have been sitting on my bed for three hours, waiting for an idea of what to write. Alas, nothing is coming."

"Is that what you have been doing all morning?" asked Ash.

I smiled, "Yes."

Mother stood back looking at the tree, "An idea is what you seek? Hmmm, well, think of your favorite things."

"I have been, though cannot seem to put even two things together."

"Have faith that something will come to

you. Elohim will give you an idea if you ask. Besides, you are a granddaughter of the Alpha. You will think of something."

I gazed to the West end of the room at a picture above the fireplace. My Grandfather, the Alpha Commander, also known as the Black Wolf, stood with my Grandmother, the Alpha Captain. Grandfather, who is leader of Elohim's army, is a full angel who can become a wolf. He held his gold sword, Ethril, which seemed to gleam through the photo. My grandmother was beautifully dressed in her usual white hooded robes, with gold hair as bright as the sun.

"Furith ik kurthith," said Alezandra standing with her feet tangled in lights.

Food, these were welcomed words to my ears. Alezandra spoke only in the Angelic language of our Grandfather since the day she was born. I had not even noticed, but sitting in my room all morning had caused me to become quite hungry. So my sister saying there was food in the kitchen made my mouth salivate. I walked down a small hallway to the kitchen to find two pancakes on a griddle waiting for me. Coming to the long table in the dining room I sat down.

As I ate, my mind drifted to another world. Images began engulfing my mind. A castle, a field, trees waving their branches in the wind coming down from nearby mountains. A hummingbird flying from branch to branch, trying to make a nest. A mouse scurries to dig a home for its family. An eagle flying in the sky looking for food. A princess in the castle waiting for her prince on a white horse as he rides along the road.

As these images ran through my head, dark clouds approached, suddenly everything became completely black. It was as if someone had taken a paint brush and with one stroke everything became black. It was the same darkness from my dream. As I wondered what this could be and where it came from I saw two bright red eyes shine through the clouds as if staring right at me.

Just then I heard a voice, I opened my eyes to see a white wolf with blue snowflake like eyes, at the doorway to the room. I blinked several times coming back to the real world, my heart beating fiercely. I had not even heard Jenna come down as she helped Alezandra.

"Hello," I said with a smile trying not to think of the black clouds in my vision. The sound of the wolf's voice had caused me to jump and drop my fork on the floor. The wolf slowly transformed into my mother.

"You are thinking hard. Your eyes have been closed for nearly ten minutes."

I bent down and picked up the fork. I finished the food on my plate then stood up and put my empty plate on the counter.

"Still thinking of an idea, nothing yet."

My mother smiled. She was a beautiful lady of, yes, four hundred years. But she still appeared thirty. Her long Blond hair as my father would often say, was eyed as gold jasper. Father always said she was the gem of his life.

"You know," said Mother sitting at the table, "when you were born, I knew right away you would be a writer. I was not wrong. You have a gift, now; let Elohim show you what to do with that gift. Don't think of the idea; let Him show it to you. You have amazed me with other stories you have written before."

I leaned back against the counter that separated the kitchen and dining room. Those were words I had to let sink in for a while.

"How did you get your powers?" I asked her.

"I was born with them. At first I was scared. When I was five, I wondered how I was making snow from my hands. I did not know why and it scared me. As I grew older I learned how to use them, but I was still frightened. When your father came to Ireland in 1977, he taught me to not be afraid. As he trained me, my powers grew. It was not long before I joined the NightWolves, as the Winter Wolf. I remember it as if it were yesterday."

"What?"

"Your father and my wedding. I wore the same robes I do today."

"Those robes are beyond ancient," I laughed.

Mother smiled, "They are the mark of the Winter Wolf. White robes like snow."

"Like Grandmother."

"A little, she wears white robes, but Grand-mother Amanda is a lot stronger than I."

"What was it like, when father met you?"

"I have told you this story many times Ez."

"I know, but it's one of my favorites."

Mother took a deep breath, "It was love at first sight for him. When he saw my powers for the first time he knew I had to be trained."

Mother opened her hands as a white saber appeared on them. This was Ith'Rain the Snow Rapier. The blade was white as snow. It was formed by my Grandmother.

"But father did not know anything about ice powers, did he?"

"I found it rather funny at times that he did not, yet wanted to help me. But I soon realized he was teaching me not to be afraid rather than how to use my powers. So, through him saying not to be afraid, I gained control of the snow and ice."

"Wintervale Cave."

"Yes, the biggest thing I ever created with my powers, April 10th, 1977."

"And the same cave we use today for Riven and Rowen."

Mother laughed, "Yes, the WolfDragons love it. It is just big enough for them to fit in."

"You have made much more than just that."

"Yes, too much to mention right now."

I noticed a WolfDragon shadow outside the window as I gazed out.

"I hope, someday, someone will look at me

the way Father saw you."

Mother took my hands turning me to her, "I feel, Ezeryah, that day will come, sooner than you think."

She turned to a clock on the wall by the kitchen entrance, "Goodness, I feel I shall start rambling. Best go find your father and the rest of your sisters, we are going to decorate the tree and will be ready soon for the star. And don't forget your Crystal Ice."

I smiled and hugged her and getting my grey robe and boots, went outside to the snow, thinking I could get some ideas out there as well. Snowflakes fell gracefully on my face as the land was already covered by seven inches of snow. I was sure my mom was not responsible for it, being the Winter Wolf and all.

When the wolf howls, the snow falls down. White is the Winter Night. It makes a frozen land, purer than ocean sand.

This rhyme flowed through my mind. Its words spoke of my mother, Lady of Winter.

Coming to the sprinkler I turned the knob. Water spayed out from five holes in two grey hoses that were lined in a straight path. The hoses were set seven feet apart from each other. Walking in between them letting the water hit me until I was soaked. But instead of freezing me in a block of ice, the water formed a very thin layer of ice crystals around my clothes and face. This was developed by my mother several years ago. The layer of ice protected us from the harsh winter winds.

Though one can move and feel things, it was mostly meant as armor to keep one warm. All except our mother who did not need it as she survives in the cold. When one comes into a warm place, it doesn't melt, it's more like vapor that appears then quickly vanishes.

The air was still, though, I could smell the smoke coming from the chimney. I saw a large shadow on the ground. I looked up to see a great WolfDragon with white fur flying among the trees. It had a string of lights in its mouth. It was circling the trees that were around the house, laying the lights perfectly within the branches from top to bottom. The WolfDragon landed on the ground and I heard the voice of Hailey.

"Perfect Rowen, this looks great."

"The trees look fantastic!" I called out as I walked towards them.

Hailey turned and waved at me. She was dressed in her grey robes with a white stripe down either side, which covered her grey armor. A grey hood covered her face, revealing only a little of her long auburn hair.

"Thanks, we are almost done. Father said yesterday he wanted forty trees covered in lights around the house this year."

A gust of wind pushed a cloud of snow at her face. Hailey reached out her right hand and pushed the cloud back with her own wind powers.

"Ten more than last year," I laughed.

Rowen turned his great WolfDragon head

towards me.

"A lot easier to decorate when one can fly," he smiled.

The WolfDragon's head was a wolf while its body was a dragon. Instead of scales the body was fur. I thought back to when my sisters found the WolfDragons. I was only five years old. Not on purpose, but they were found as eggs.

I looked back at the house. It was nicely decorated.

"Well, carry on," I said turning back to them.

"Are they ready for the star yet?"

"No, they are still getting the lights on the tree."

"I saw mom and Ash cutting it this morning. A good size."

"Indeed. Do you happen to know where dad is?"

Hailey pointed south towards the forest, "He went to The Glade a couple hours ago." She turned back to her WolfDragon, "Alright, we got two trees left. Let's do this."

I walked away as Rowen lifted into the air and took off. I kept looking at our house with the décor. Our house was not quite a castle, though some would say it is. There were thirteen rooms and three stories. It was made of strong oak. Father built it not long after I was born.

There were four towers on the West, East, North, and South corners of the house. One of those towers was Jenna and my room of the very top. Another was Father's office. The South was Alezandra and Heather's room. The last one was a library. Each tower was made from red brick.

We called it Alnor Wik, which means, House of Light in Angelic. It has a light almost like a lighthouse on the roof. It was so those in danger could come here for safety. It was always on no matter what. The house was set on a small hill with mountains to the North and ocean to the South.

The city of Glenarm was to the West. Glenarm was the place where my father came the first time he arrived in Ireland. The town of Limerick was to the North near the mountains. Northwest within the forest that surrounded my house was the village of Ahntharo. Here lives the entire Army of the Moon, as well as their families.

As I rounded the house to the other side I saw Katie flying on her WolfDragon Riven, dropping green and white lights around trees. Katie, or Khil in Angelic, was known as the Wolf Princess, Lady of Healing. She always wore white robes and a crown of leaves on her head. She carried a bow with which she fired gold arrows, sharper than any sword, except Grandfather's. She got her Wolf Princess title from Elohim. She is also married to Zander, the NightGuard Captain. They live in a castle near the mountains. All that is another story. It was odd that even though she is the oldest of my siblings and me, she is the second shortest next to Heather who's the youngest. I am the middle child, and the tallest.

The one thing we did not have, were cars. We had electricity, but no oil or gas for engines. Horses were our primary way of transportation. Almost two hundred and fifty years ago, the world depleted the oil of earth. Things got more and more expensive until finally, the world crumbled. I had been told by Katie, who is now fifty-four, that when she was seventeen, the world was in chaos. Nobody knew what to do. Slowly but surely the world melted back into a planet of farms and carriages pulled by horses. Oh, we still have cities, but many things now relied only on electricity and coal.

I walked towards the stables near a small frozen river. Three beautiful white horses and one black. The black was Toronto, belonging to father. It was said the name Toronto came from an Indian that Grandfather knew years earlier. The three white ones were Destiny, belonging to Jenna, Kayla, belonging to mother. My horse was Kelly, named after my late aunt. As I approached Kelly, she looked up at me with her beautiful brown eyes. I stroked the mare's great white mane.

"Good morning."

I turned towards Toronto to see my youngest sister, Heather brushing his mane.

"Good morning, dear sister," I said.

She wore blue robes that seemed to have streams of water flowing through it. Four small fangs hung from the corners of her mouth. She was half human, half wolf. She could become a wolf, but as a human, she was part canine. Her fangs also messed up her words every time she spoke.

"I hear the Army of the Moon are coming for thinner."

"Yes, Voldar's Reeth is in a week. Father wants them over every night."

"Doethn't he ehery year?"

We both laughed.

"True," I replied petting Kelly's neck. "Ash and mother are getting the lights on the tree now. It is nearly time."

Heather put down her brush and picked up a bucket.

"Good, almoth thime for the thar."

I watched as she put her hand over the bucket and water began to appear. Soon the bucket was full. She carried it over to the horse trough and filled it. I loved her River Wolf powers.

"I hear father is in The Glade in the forest."

"Yeth. He came by earlier ath I wath waking the hortheth. He ith practhing thord play."

I thanked her and continued walking to the forest. Upon entry, I instantly felt the warmth of the trees as they shaded the harsh cold from outside. There was barely any snow beneath the trees. Once in a while a squirrel ran from tree to tree. As I walked there were sounds of metal ahead of me.

Chapter 3
The Drawing and a Message

I arrived in a clearing in the middle of the forest. Eight pillars of grey stone lined The Glade in a circle. In the middle of the space was a man dressed in dark green cloth. A hooded cloak hid his face. In his right hand was a small but thick looking stick. The man stood impeccably still as breath like frost emerged from his mouth.

As I watched from a distance a blade shot out from each side of the stick. He jumped into the air twirling the sword like helicopter blades. If there had been someone in front of him, they would have been in pieces. He landed perfectly on the ground slicing a stuffed dummy cleanly in half. I clapped as he rose to his feet.

"Welcome, my daughter."

I walked up to him eyeing the dummy on the ground as Father turned to me. A silver wolf face was on his black breastplate as well as his shoulders. Four white fangs shined from all corners of his mouth when he opened it. But unlike Heather, Father's speech was clear.

"You must teach me that."

"I serve Elohim and Emmanuel, as well as my father, I have been trained to fight, and to use my skills to protect the world."

"I have much to learn, don't I?"

My father laughed and replied, "Soon, you shall know the moves of the Beta Captain. So on this glorious and cold day, what can I do for you?"

"Almost time for the star on the tree."

"Good, anything else?"

I had not thought about why else I was here, but asked, "What are dreams?"

"What do you mean?"

"Like what are they to you?"

Father stuck his sword in the ground and sat on a nearby log, his fog like breath becoming more intense.

"You are old enough to know the answer."

"Dad, I must know your answer."

With a deep breath he replied, "Well, dreams can be many things. Good dreams, bad dreams, some could even be a vision."

"What kind of vision?"

"A vision could also be anything. A memory, from the past, sometimes even something of what is to come."

I sat on the ground by a pillar.

"Ez, why do you ask me of this? Have you had a vision?"

My eyes narrowed to the slain dummy,

"I...I have dreams, a lot, as you know, each time wondering if any are trying to tell me something."

Father smiled, "Pray about this, let Elohim show you the answer. You have had many visions several that have saved lives in the past."

I stood and hugged my father.

"Want to tell me about these dreams?"

My mind thought fast as I let him go. To tell him about last night, or the past week?

"Oh no, not right now."

As I watched snowflakes fall to the ground, my mind wandered again.

"I love this time of year."

Father turned to me, "Why? It's cold."

"But it is peaceful. Nature sleeps at the moment. I feel at peace."

Father smiled, "I wish it was like that in the world."

"We all do, Father."

He gazed up at the sky as snowflakes landed gracefully on his face.

"I have seen many things, fought many battles. The way the world is rotating, I fear peace will never come. I wish life could be like a snowflake, it does not rush, it is gentle and calm, it simply falls, it is beautiful."

"Unless it is a blizzard."

I heard Father chuckle at my remark.

"This world is like a blizzard, rushing here and there, not always able to see where it is going. But a gentle snowflake, slow and steady." He took my hand holding it flat in the air as a single snowflake fell gently onto my palm, "is what the world needs to be."

I smiled at the sight while putting my other hand on Father's shoulder so he faced me.

"We must take each day that we are not fighting a battle as a day of peace. Each moment we are not fighting, is a moment of peace."

Father smiled, "You will be a great writer someday."

"I only hope so, Father."

At that moment, a vision entered my head. Darkness, a forest in the night, a path, thick tall trees as an eerie fog settled in. Suddenly out of the shadows of the trees a figure appeared, the same one from my nightmare. As the red eyes flashed open, I jumped. I had snapped from the vision, my father had his back to me. I shook my head, trying to focus on the real world. As my eyes cleared, I got an idea.

"Father?"

He turned to me, "Yes?"

"You know those stories, of the Great Battle? The ones you tell me about."

"Yes. Four hundred years ago, your Angelic grandfather led the charge of thousands of soldiers against Cain, leader of The Dark Flames."

At the mention of Dark Flames, I realized it was the army from my dream.

"You were there."

Father sighed, "I was. I remember that demon well. He was seven feet tall. His red eyes could pierce the very soul like fire. Black horns on his black iron helmet that reminded you of the

Dark Prince."

Red eyes? Black horns? My dream came to full view in my mind.

"Can you draw me a picture of what Cain looked like?"

Father's eyes never left me, "Why?"

"You have told me in the past, but I want to see for myself."

Father sat on the log again and opened his hand as a pencil and paper appeared on the palm. He drew for a few minutes.

After awhile, "Best I can do."

He handed it to me as I extended a quaking hand to take the paper.

"Ez, are you alright?"

I steadied myself and gently took the drawing. "Yes, sorry."

I slowly lowered my head to a dreadful sight. The picture was not perfect, but it was enough to make me gasp quietly. The figure in the drawing was that of what I saw in my nightmare, and every vision sense. I felt my bones shake inside my body, trembling and weakness engulfed my legs. I felt my heart skip a beat, maybe several. I looked up at my father trying not to appear frightened.

"Father, do you think he is gone forever?"

Before he could answer a dark green armored rider on a black horse approached stopping a few yards away from us. Noticing the bandana that covered his face, I knew it was a NightWolf. The rider got off the horse and pulled away his dark green hood to reveal the NightWolf Captain, he quickly saluted us.

"Ah, Delthar," said Father. "What do we owe the honor of..."

The Captain interrupted, "Sir, We do not have much time. Gather everyone in your house. I have a message for you all."

† † †

"What?!" cried father.

We were all gathered in the Middle Room of the house as Delthar explained his story. A roaring fire was crackling in the fireplace.

"Yes, Captain, the demons are going to attack here, at dawn."

"How did you come by this?"

"A messenger of Elohim came to us at the Village."

"So close to the Celebration of Voldar's Reeth," said Jenna who was in her white wolf form, her watch hanging around her neck. She had brown fur around her eyes which were also brown.

"Sy kerth rhey ederlik ga (Why must they attack now)?" asked Alezandra.

"I don't know," Delthar nodded.

"When thith war end, I will danth, becauth I will be free thu withouth fear."

"Da nar u (I'm with you)," Alezandra replied smiling at Heather.

Both girls were the dancers of the family. If Celtic music was ever played, they danced no matter where they were.

"This war will end," said Father taking Alezandra's hands. "For I want to see you all have the chance to do what you want, without fear of evil."

Mother stood up and walked to him.

"Can you sense who is leading this demonic army?"

Father came to the middle of the room and crossing his right hand to his heart, closed his eyes. This was my father in deep meditation. After a few minutes, he opened them and looked around at us.

"Well?" asked Ash sitting on the couch with Heather and me.

"It is not who is leading them. It is what."

My siblings and I shot each other concerned looks.

"A ghost knight."

"A ghost knight?" asked Katie.

"It is leading an army of demons. At least, it will be."

"Dark Flames?" I asked.

Every head turned towards me. My father took a deep breath.

"I...I don't know. Is there something you want to tell me?"

I shook my head no.

"Just a thought."

I did not want to tell him about the dream, not yet.

"I suppose it is a possibility," said mother.

"But Grandfather, he destroyed them. He destroyed The Dark Flames, in the Great Battle," said Jenna. "Didn't he?"

Father looked at Delthar who nodded.

"We must be ready for anything," he said looking back at us. "But I will say to be rest assured, The Dark Flames, are not returning."

We all nodded. Father turned back to Delthar.

"Gather the entire Army of the Moon in the White Fortress."

Delthar saluted him then turned to the door. Father glanced back to us.

"Begin your training, we must be ready at a moment's notice."

"I can set up the targets for arrows," said Katie.

"Anything we do to prepare. But first go to your castle, WolfHaven, find Zander and the NightGuards, bring them. And find Riven."

"Right away, Father."

"I will find Rowen, as he cannot be far," said Hailey.

Ash nodded his head, "I will contact Cedric. He will help."

"My wather powerth will only freethe in winther's grathp," said Heather next to me.

Alezandra extended a hand as a tiny flame danced on her palm, "Uthan de Mahro fes-olaz rask." (Perhaps my fire can help-with that)

Jenna took the watch from her neck in her paw, "I shall make sure my watch is working properly, just in case."

As we dispersed, Hailey turned to me, "Why do you think it is The Dark Flames?"

I thought about the question as I sat staring into space, shifting my eyes to her, "I don't know."

† † †

Thirty minutes later, I sat on my bed rolling my pencil in my hand. I'd hidden the drawing Father made under my pillow.

"Still no ideas?"

I turned to Jenna coming into the room still as a wolf. I smiled.

"No."

The truth was I was not thinking of a story, but the dream. Jenna hopped onto my bed next to me. I petted the fur on her back. I saw the small pocket watch around her neck, ticking.

"I feel I need an adventure to give me an idea."

"We are about to go on one."

I could sense concern in my sister's voice as she was right to feel that way.

"Are you afraid?"

She turned to me.

"Are you?"

I thought about those words. I had been through many battles with demons. But the thought of The Dark Flames returning scared me. Then again, maybe these were different demons. I had not met The Dark Flames, but from my father's stories, I did not want to. Nor did I want to meet their demonic leader. But what of my dream? Could somebody be telling me something? It was all that had been in my head. It was still fresh.

"I'm trying not to be," I answered.

"I wish I could go to a time that was peaceful," I heard Jenna say.

I took her paw in my hand.

"You could. You are the Time Wolf."

Jenna looked down at the bed.

"True, I did go to 1335 yesterday. Not a very peaceful time."

I laughed as she turned and hopped to the floor, transformed into a human and walked to her window, looking out at the snow land.

"I can't wait until this war is over."

I smiled, "Nor can I. I feel everyone has the same feeling."

"Grandfather has wanted it for hundreds of years."

I smiled as I thought about Grandfather. The great warrior had fought so many battles against demons, he could write several books of his own life.

Just then I heard thunderous sounds outside. We both looked out my window to see hundreds of riders on black horses approach our house. The Army of the Moon had arrived.

Chapter 4
Telling of the Dream

Father called an emergency meeting. I came to a great fortress to the west of the house. Ok, it was more a Church than a fortress. An underground Church. First there were four walls of white marble that formed a square. A tall steeple of the same stone stood in the middle. An entrance led to a flight of stairs departing down. Above the doors on the white stone was a large brown wooden cross. At the entrance stood two big NightGuards in green battle armor their swords drawn.

I walked down the grey stairs into a large room. I looked around as the Moon Soldiers gathered in what we called the Moon Den. The Moon Den was a huge square room with four torches lining each wall. The walls and ceiling were made of dark grey stone. The floor was of oak wood. Four pillars made a smaller square in the middle of the room.

A stone, four and a half feet high was in the very center of the room. On the front of the stone were these words in Angelic:

"Derac le a vithgi Ta Kitaka tor Min Zax, Lungrire" (Gather in the name of Elohim and His Son, Emmanuel).

A book lay open on the stone. Hundreds of chairs encircled the stone. This was where we had service on Sundays and Wednesdays, or where we came to pray and meditate.

The book was open to my favorite verse in the Scriptures: Hebrews 11:1, Now faith is the substance of things hoped for, the evidence of things not seen.

These were words I lived by. They had helped me throughout my life. As I entered the room, Edward, greeted me with a smile as he sat on a black chair near the entrance.

"How are you?"

"I am well," I replied.

He is a kind yet mysterious man, who was very good with a bow and arrow. He is also the Captain of the NightFangs. Like all Moon Soldiers, he wore a dark green hooded cloak over black armor. His bow and quiver hung around his back. The bow was of dark oak wood while the riser was silver.

It was Edward who saved my life years ago. A state called Colorado in America, on a mountain called Pikes Peak, in a city called Colorado Springs. I had come to battle my mortal enemy Vestus, who almost killed me, if not for Edward fatally shooting him with an arrow.

Next to Edward was Jack, a NightGuard, sitting, twirling his sword on the wood floor.

His dark green metal helmet rested on the floor next to him. He was the most Irish looking with a red goatee and a small red mustache.

Next to him was Ryan a Nightwolf. Beside him were Matthias, his brother, and Captain of the NightHunters. Next was Luke, a NightWolf and the brains for most missions. I expected him to talk quite a bit during this gathering.

A bigger man stood near the entrance to the room holding a great zweihander, it was Zander. He was dressed in full battle armor as he normally was, while his metal helmet was in the shape of a wolf head. A stone wolf head sat on either shoulder, the mark of the captain, same with Edward, Delthar, Matthias and Samuel.

Next to him was Felix, a NightFang. These were the original NightWolves when my father first came, at least these were what was left of the originals.

The rest of the soldiers filed into the room. Since my father came here almost five hundred years ago, the Army of the Moon had grown close to nine hundred. Even several women had combined with them. But the majority was still clearly men.

The room was soon filled and I sat down next to Edward. Delthar stood and led the Anthem of Elohim. It was customary to sing a song before Church or any kind of assembly. I loved hearing the voices of everyone. I could easily pick out my father's voice from the crowd, as it was the deepest.

RETURN OF THE BLACK KNIGHT

"Over High Mountains,
through deep seas,
we march to battle.
With Elohim in the lead,
we fight for morning's dawn.
The moonlight shines,
guiding our way,
to the break of day.
With our banner held high,
and our hands to the sky,
let us shout for victory,
today and ever more.
With swords drawn,
and arrows strung,
we fight til we've won.

"Faith is stronger than fear.
And we wipe away every tear,
for those that die, live on.
And when we have won,
we ring the bells of victories song.

"Hearts high, a road long,
we ride to battle.
With our eyes to the skies,
we fight til the day is done.
The line is drawn, we stand firm,
to the dark of night.
With swords held high,
and our shouts to the sky,
let us sing the anthem, of Elohim.
With weapons in hand,
we make our stand, til we've won."

After the song was over, Father stood and came to the stone.

"Welcome everyone," he started. "It is good to see you all here. Though I wish it was under better circumstances."

Delthar stood next to Father with both arms crossed.

"You all know why we are here," he said. "We don't know exactly what we will be facing."

"When will the enemy arrive?" asked a NightWolf.

"According to Delthar, tomorrow morning."

Jenna was sitting next to me. I looked over at her, she seemed a bit puzzled by my face. The dream was nagging at me again.

"Are you alright?"

"I'm fine," I said.

"What is it?" she asked quietly.

I took a deep breath, as my head was starting to hurt.

"I'm not sure."

"So I will just tell you to be prepared," I heard father say. "Luke and I will begin a plan on how to defeat this enemy. My friends, we have fought many battles, and we will win this one. Delthar, Edward, Zander, Matthias, Samuel, get your men together. Begin training. May the knights in all of us be pure and strong. Now, who will go to Glenarm to make safe the city?"

It was almost an instant response, "Here I am Beta Captain, send me. My NightBlades are ready and waiting."

"Good, Captain Samuel will go."

Samuel at once left the building with dozens of soldiers behind him.

All the Moon Soldiers began talking and murmuring. I couldn't take it anymore, I nudged Jenna to follow me.

† † †

We arrived in our room a few minutes later.

As Jenna closed the door she turned to me, "Ez, what's wrong?"

I stood in front of my window staring into space.

"To be honest, I really don't know."

My heart was pounding fast, I put my hand on my chest to calm it. Jenna sat on her bed and waited for me to continue.

"I had a dream."

I turned to face my sister who seemed interested.

"I'm not sure what it means. But it has been the same dream for a week."

"Is it about the demons?"

"Maybe, but I'm so confused."

I sat down on my bed as Jenna scooted closer.

"I think I saw him."

"Who do you mean?"

"It...It was...Cain."

Jenna turned pale.

"Are you sure?"

"It was a knight with red eyes, just as Grandfather has told us. You came to warn me of an attack, that's when I saw him."

Jenna stared at me.

"I'm sure it was just a dream, right?"

I tried to smile, but couldn't. But a thought still lingered.

"Then how did I know about The Dark Flames earlier?"

Jenna sat back. She moved her eyes back and forth. I could tell she was thinking hard.

"You have a good point. But...it's not possible. Cain has been dead for over four hundred years. You know the tale."

"I had a vision earlier too. I was trying to think of an idea to write. I saw dark clouds, black clouds, as black as can be. I saw his eyes. Thankfully mom came into the room before I could see more."

Jenna shivered. I took her hands.

"We know the stories that Grandfather tells us. Four hundred years ago was the Great Battle. Four hundred thousand Flames against Grandfather's ten thousand soldiers. During the battle Grandfather knocked the evil knight into an endless hole."

"We must tell Father."

Jenna stood but I caught her hand.

"No, we can't."

"What? Ez, this is Cain we are..."

"And have father freak out?"

Jenna turned to me.

"Jen, you know that it was because of Cain

that Aunt Kelly and Uncle Max died. It tore Father apart. If we tell him he is certainly going to lose it, and we don't need that. I can't bear the thought of what he would do if he found out."

Jenna walked to her window.

"Your right. We never knew Kelly, but from the stories Father told us...he cried when he told them."

"That is why we can't tell him. Besides, this may have just been a dream I had."

"I hope your right. But if it's not?"

I took a deep breath, "Then we are all in real danger. Will you help me?"

"You want my help?"

"I can't do this alone. We must find clues, anything to tell us the truth."

Jenna took my hand in hers, "Yes, Sister, I shall help."

Just then there was a knock on the door. Jenna opened it to find Edward. We welcomed him in and he stood before us.

"You left the meeting rather quick. Your father, Cody sent me to find you. I am to bring you both to begin training in The Glade."

Jenna shot me a glance.

"Can we at least tell him?"

I had to think about that. Would it be good to let him in on the dream?

"Tell me what?" Edward asked.

I sighed.

"Can you keep a secret?"

"Of-course. I mean, it depends on what it

is. But we need to meet with your father."

I took a deep breath. Training would have to wait.

"I had a dream last night."

Edward turned to me, "Go on."

Jenna sat on her bed across from me.

"Well, I don't know what it means exactly. But I saw Cain."

Edward looked like he might choke on his own saliva.

"Cain?" he said quietly.

"Yes," I replied.

Edward's eyes darted between me and Jenna as he leaned against a desk.

"Are you sure, like one hundred percent?"

"Maybe ninety."

The archer took a deep breath then smiled, "Let us not fret over a dream. Come, we must meet your father for training."

He walked to the door, "Are you not even the least bit curious?" asked Jenna.

Edward turned to her, "Should I be?"

I stood, walked to my pillow, taking the drawing Father drew from underneath. I handed it to Edward with a shaking hand, he gazed down to the drawing of Cain.

"Where did you get this?" he asked walking back to the desk, eyes glued to the red eyed knight in the picture.

"Father drew it for me this morning. This is what I saw."

After a few seconds of looking it over, "I'm sure it was just a dream," he said closing the front cover. "Where in it did you see him?"

"WinterFang."

"The forest?"

"It was a path."

"Fox Trail is the only road from here to Glenarm. The only road that cuts through the forest."

"Father said it was a ghost knight attacking tomorrow," said Jenna. "Could it be possible Cain is that ghost knight?"

"It is impossible. I was in the Great Battle all those years ago. Cain's army was in the hundreds of thousands. We were on the brink of destruction. Many good soldiers fell that day. Wolf and Cain in an intense duel. I saw the demon fall into that endless pit. He is gone forever. I am convinced of this."

"You would have lost without the Spirit Wolves."

"Yes. Like I said, defeat was imminent. But then your Grandfather said those words, and four thousand spirits appeared. We did win because of them."

I stood and walked to Jenna's window.

"Did you notice anything that would indicate a return?" she asked behind me.

"No."

"We have to be sure. It is too much of a coincidence, the dream, an attack. It is all too perfect."

"Have you had a dream with him in it before?" Edward asked me.

"This whole week. But before that, nothing."

I felt Edward put a hand on my shoulder.

"Let's tell your father."

"No," I said turning to face him. "If we tell him he will lose it. And possibly attack Cain on his own."

"Edward you know how much he misses Kelly," said Jenna. "And you know how much it tore him apart when Kelly died. I mean, sure it wasn't Aunt Hannah, but still."

Edward nodded in agreement.

"I am quite glad it was not Hannah. They have been best friends since birth. Cody would have attacked Cain on his own had she been killed. And no one has heard from your Uncle Rudolph or Aunt Karen in almost a hundred years. I feel there is much eating at him."

"It was years ago, sixty to be exact, since they both vanished," I replied. "Neither Jenna or I were born."

"Not to mention your cousin Matt. As far as we know he is still fighting in Japan."

"So, what do we do?" asked Jenna standing to her feet.

I stood next to her.

"This is a puzzle, I feel we will need to find the pieces to complete the mystery. We must figure out what is going on. If Cain has truly returned, or is going to, we are in immense danger."

"We do not have an army to fight The Dark Flames," said Edward.

"We have to try."

Jenna turned to him, "Try that which is

meant to be tried."

"Exactly," I replied.

Jenna turned again to the archer, "Are you with us?"

The captain sat on a chair near the desk, staring into space.

"Why do you want to do this? Like you said, it could just be a dream."

I took a deep breath, "Because I'm scared."

He smiled.

"I don't blame you. But how do you know it was Cain in your dream? It is hard for me to comprehend all this. Sorry to continue asking."

"We all know this story. Cain, he who wears black armor from head to toe, red eyes that pierce like fire, the hooked horns on his helmet. That is what I saw. Fire seemed to follow him. He came from the shadows like a ghost, with an army behind him."

Edward stared at me and took a deep breath.

"Everyone will wonder where we are."

Turning to Jenna I saw the watch around her neck, "Not if time stops. We can freeze the world."

"I have to anyway," said Jenna.

I remembered what Grandfather had said years back, "If you go traveling in the past, you must freeze the present. If you do not, your future gets erased once you leave. Freeze it, to keep it."

Jenna was right, as usual.

"But will that stop Cain?" asked Edward

looking up at her. "Remember we are not your grandfather. I don't have powers like you, but can you stop the Black Knight?"

Jenna looked at me with a concerned face. Edward was right, I knew he was. Grandfather was at least fifty times stronger than us. There were not many who could beat him in a duel. On a power scale he was probably a five hundred, while I was only at a thirty. But did we have a choice? There was only one.

"We have to try," I said. "If we can freeze Cain, we could stop him from attacking while we are gone."

"Let us depart in ten minutes," said Jenna

"Where to first?" asked Edward.

I thought about that.

"Why not all the places that Cain and Grandfather ever met, ever talked, ever fought?"

I smiled at the idea.

"Jenna, you are a genius."

"The pyramids in Egypt," replied Edward. "From the stories, your grandfather first met Cain there."

Jenna turned to me.

"The pyramids it is," I replied. "Jenna, wait a few minutes before you freeze the world."

"You got it."

Edward rose to his feet.

"Time travel. We can travel to the different places where Wolf is with Cain."

I nodded, it was a brilliant idea.

"At least enough times until we find an adequate amount of clues to turn into answers."

"Perfect," said Jenna. "A time travelling adventure."

"We will need money to pay for things, if needed," said Edward.

I went to my bed pulling out a small chest from under it. Opening it I took a bag tossing it to Edward. The NightFang smiled at the sight of the gold coins. I then pulled out from under my bed, the box that held my sword. I gripped it tightly.

"With this sword, I will right all wrong."

Jenna bent under her bed and lifted her sword in her hands. It had three small clocks within the blade on both sides. It was known as the time sword even though the hands of the clocks did not move. She held it out to me.

"I'm with you."

Edward took an arrow from his quiver strapping it to his bow.

"As am I."

I smiled.

"Let's do this." A thought entered, "Hold on, maybe we should tell someone."

"Like who?" asked Jenna.

"Mom."

"You know your mother had a big run in with the Black Knight years ago," replied Edward. "It might be good to at least tell her."

"Exactly, prepare yourselves, I shall return," I then vanished.

Chapter 5

Preparing to Leave

I appeared outside the White Fortress as Moon Soldiers continued to file out. I spotted Mother coming out from the Moon Den.

"Mother!"

She smiled at me, "My darling daughter, what is it?"

"I must in private speak with you."

"Sounds important?"

"Very."

Mother motioned for me to follow.

We settled on the stone seats in the den, I was relieved we were alone.

"Now," Mother began, "what is it?"

I took a deep breath, "This morning when Father said a ghost knight was attacking tomorrow, and I said, The Dark Flames."

"Have you had a vision of them returning?"

Yes, last night. I mean I had a vision of them, but I don't know what it means. Do you think Cain could return?"

Mother turned looking at the floor, "I had

said this morning that it is possible, only hoping it is not. I was with Cain for a while. I saw the things he could do."

"Jenna, Edward and I want to find clues."

"And you should," Mother replied standing up to face me. "There are many things you do not know of Cain. You had the dream, now go, solve the mystery."

"I will not fail you."

"I know you won't Ez, but I feel something is coming, something we cannot see, not yet."

† † †

As the moments passed by, I closed my eyes as Edward and I huddled with Jenna in our room.

I was dressed in my grey hooded robe, with a grey long sleeve shirt underneath and a white t-shirt over that. Grey silk and leather pants stretched down to my grey leather boots which had two straps of metal armor around each. Jenna was in her brown hooded robe with black leather boots. A black belt was strapped around her black silk pants while her robe hid a black and brown shirt. Both of us had our swords strapped to our belts. Edward remained in his green hooded cape with black armor underneath and black leather boots.

As Jenna took her watch in her hands she pressed a single knob on the side. I opened my eyes and listened, silence. Was time halted?

Edward stood and slowly opened the

bedroom door and looked around.

"You may want to see this."

Jenna and I stood up noticing everyone except us was frozen. I turned to my companions.

"Come on."

"Where?" asked Jenna as I moved towards Father's office.

"The scrolls," I replied.

Edward walked in after me, "What scrolls?"

"Father keeps a few scrolls in a small box, they contain verses that may be able to help us."

Father's office was a small library with an oak desk in the middle. The place smelled of books which is why I loved coming in here. I would come borrow a book and read in a green chair by a window at the corner of the room. I found the box and opened it to find four small scrolls.

"Why do we need these exactly?" asked Jenna standing by the door.

While looking through the parchment I replied, "Do you remember five years ago, there was the Battle of Madrid? Before the fight began, Father read these to us. It was almost like it strengthened us, because we won. Just in case we need some strengthening."

"I do remember."

Pulling out a scroll the string tied around it fell off and the paper unraveled. It opened to Ephesians 6:10-20. Reading it made me smile.

"We have our armor?"

"We do," said Edward.

"Swords?"

"Check," said Jenna holding hers.

I put the scroll back in the box taking only two.

"Now we grab any food and supplies we will need. We must travel light enough that we will still move quickly."

Jenna instantly ran downstairs to the kitchen. Edward and I slowly came down to the statues of people in the Middle Room. I spotted Father near Grandfather's picture, frozen with Delthar and Mother. I turned to Edward.

"Get some Fire Leaves from the storage closet by the back door."

As Edward left I glanced back at the giant picture on the wall. I stared at Grandfather's face which seemed to move, speaking to me. I felt a voice calling me, it sounded like his, but it was faint, almost un-able to be heard.

"Find him."

That was all I could hear. Find Cain? Or someone else? I was not sure. I turned to see Edward as he carried a backpack into the room.

"Jenna went to get the horses unfrozen, so we can take them with us."

I looked back at the picture.

"We have to find Cain, alive or dead."

Edward put a hand on my shoulder.

"We will find out what's going on."

I sat down next to Heather who was on the couch frozen. She had been talking to Ash who was standing next to her. I waved a hand in her face then glanced at my brother. Neither of them blinked.

"I can't let anything happen to them."

Edward smiled.

"That is why you have us."

Looking around at everyone frozen, I had always enjoyed it when Jenna used her powers. It was also weird seeing my family and the army like this. It felt like a wax museum. I noticed Edward go to Heather's other side. Her left arm was raised and her index finger was pointing at Ash. Edward gently pushed her arm and hand to the couch.

"At least having the world like this now, will give us time to see the past."

I nodded as the back door closed and Jenna came into the room.

"Ready?"

I stood to my feet.

"Yes. Let's do this."

Edward stood up, "Horses ready?"

"Yes, Destiny and Kelly are anxious for a run."

"I suspect Ethkar (Edward's horse) is also." (Ethkar means Friend)

I walked up to Father and gave him a hug, "We will find out what is going on."

"And we are going to the Pyramids first right?" inquired Jenna.

"Yes," I replied turning and walking to the back door covering my head with the hood.

On my way out, I passed by Alezandra who stood in the kitchen with an apple to her mouth. I gently took the apple from her hand and continued to the door.

RETURN OF THE BLACK KNIGHT

I walked outside to see Riven frozen in the sky with Katie riding him. Hailey and Rowen were near the West corner of the house. Hailey was dressed in her gray robes and had her hand out to the WolfDragon with a small ice cube resting on her palm. I walked up to them and waved a hand in Hailey's face.

Rowen had his mouth open to take the ice. WolfDragons are ice dragons that breathe frost fire. Not hot, but incase targets in ice, or impale them with icicles. I gazed to the sky at the snowflakes frozen in midflight.

I spotted twelve NightFangs halted while shooting arrows at targets in the snow. The arrows were frozen in midflight. We came to where our three horses were grazing through the snow. Finding any grass in this much snow was like finding a needle in a haystack.

I climbed onto Kelly and stroked her left ear. I took the reins as Edward and Jenna mounted their horses.

A thought entered my mind.

"We cannot take the horses."

Jenna turned stunned, "What do you mean?"

"There will be times we will not need them, and what if we leave them behind in another time?"

Jenna opened her mouth to speak, but paused, "Good point."

"So, what do we do with them?" asked Edward stroking his horse.

"I would feel terrible to freeze them again."

I shook my head, "Leave them be, they will

be fine. Besides it should not take us too long."

"But will they not be erased when we leave?" inquired Edward.

Jenna shook her head, this was true. The three horses soon stood perfectly still.

I stroked Kelly's mane, "Sorry old girl, we will be back soon."

"Well, work that watch and let's be off," said Edward.

I turned to Jenna, "Wait, let us pray for safe passage in this journey."

"An excellent idea," said Edward.

We stood together in a circle and crossing our right arms over our chests, I said, "Emmanuel, be with us in our adventure. May we find the clues that will lead us to the truth of my dream. May Your Spirit guide us. And may we not lose sight of You."

"Amen," we said together lowering our hands.

"Now, something else."

"What is it?" asked Jenna.

"We must go to WinterFang Forest. To the spot I saw Cain."

"From your dream?"

"Yes."

Edward shook his head, "What if that spot does not exist?"

"Do you think you could find it?" asked Jenna. "Edward is right, that spot may not even be there."

"Unsure am I about this, unsure about anything right now, but I can try."

Chapter 6

Another Vision

We walked along the forest floor, causing a crunch sound as our feet left snow tracks behind us. We finally came to a clearing. I walked to a tree, while transforming into a white wolf and sniffed the ground. All I got was a nose full of cold snow.

"Anything?!" called Jenna.

"Just snow," I replied.

"Anything look familiar?" I heard Edward ask.

"No."

I looked around listening carefully.

"It's here, I know it is."

"Maybe it was not even near here," Jenna called out.

I focused my eyes, I looked carefully at each tree around me.

"No, it's here, this is Fox Trail."

The wide path cut through the trees towards the city of Glenarm which I could barely make out in the distance. I walked a few more steps to a large oak tree, sniffing the ground around it. Finally, I caught a scent, an old scent, but it was something. It smelled foul.

A sudden sound like a branch cracking made me look up and listen. I saw and heard nothing. Walking a bit further, I saw a strange looking tree. There was something familiar about it.

As I neared the tree a feeling of danger arose. Was this a vision? I glanced to Jenna and Edward, but they were gone. To my left a path cut deeper into the forest. Suddenly a figure appeared in silver and black armor, and drawing a long black sword, his eyes glowing yellow. I slowly stood to my paws. I heard a voice, it was the knight's. The voice was low and deep. Knowing it was demonic, I could not make out a single word. A sudden shake woke me from the dream, looking up to see Edward.

"Are you alright?"

My right side was freezing from the snow on my fur.

"I think so."

"Did you have a vision?"

"I'm not sure, I saw something though."

"What do we do now?"

"Where is Jenna?" I asked turning back into a human.

"She is near, not to worry."

I tried to stand but fell to my knees.

"The vision has taken a lot of energy out of me."

"Come, I will help you to your sister."

As Edward helped me to my feet I saw Jenna waiting by a tree, she smiled with delight when she saw us. I hugged my sister tight.

"Are you ok?" she asked.

"Yes, but, how long was I out?"

"About seven minutes."

"At least it was not more. The longer visions require more energy."

"Well, let us pray you don't have another one like that."

"Maybe we will rest for a bit," said Edward. "We will continue when you are ready."

"Thank you," I replied.

Chapter 7

The Pyramids

After resting several minutes, I was ready to go.

I looked to my sister, "So, Jenna, do you know what year we are going to?"

She gazed at Edward for guidance.

"33 A.D.," he replied. "Wolf told me the stories several times."

"One reason I am glad to have you with us," I winked.

Jenna looked at me and grinned as she took her watch from around her neck. As Edward and I put a hand on both of her shoulders, Jenna closed her eyes and started turning the knob backwards on the watch. We both closed our eyes and felt wind rushing past us. Only by holding onto Jenna could we travel with her.

A few minutes later we opened our eyes to see three great pyramids before us. No longer were we in winter, but everything was now a desert. I knelt to feel the hot sand beneath me.

"2500 years in the past."

Jenna wrapped the watch necklace around her neck, "Where would you two be without me?"

Edward laughed.

I looked around the vast desert. After taking a few steps I turned to my companions.

"Is time moving here?"

"No, it is not," my sister replied.

"Until we find Grandfather, it might be a good idea."

"Right, let us begin," said Edward.

In all my years of life I had never been here before. I always wanted to visit. I felt around the rough sand stone of the pyramid.

"Amazing they have held up for thousands of years," I heard Jenna say behind me.

"These were made by master craftsmen," said Edward feeling the stones.

I had to agree. Not many buildings were made like this anymore. As I rounded the corner I almost bumped into someone. It was Julie, the white tiger, frozen in her human form. She was standing with her arms crossed next to an opening into the pyramid. Her sword hung around her waist. I waved a hand in her face, nothing happened, her eyes were still as stone. Edward approached the entrance of the Pyramid and peered in.

"It is pitch black."

I noticed Jenna looking at Julie.

"What is she doing out here?"

Looking around until I found tracks in the sand leading into the pyramid.

"This is where Grandfather found Ethril is it not?"

"Yes, this is the place," replied Edward, turning to me.

"Then could he be in there and Julie is standing guard out here?"

Jenna drew closer to us.

"Then they are looking for the sword right now."

I turned around where I was, gazing about the desert. All was quiet.

"I see no sign of the enemy."

"Cain may not be here yet," said Edward.

"Ezeryah, look over there."

I turned to Jenna following her gaze to a beautiful white horse standing in the sand. It was Tybalt, Grandfather's horse. The stallion could move close to one hundred mph, now he was perfectly still. I went to back to the statue of Julie with Edward behind me.

"Let us hide, once you start time, Jenna, I feel something will happen."

Jenna and I both transformed into wolves and climbed the pyramid with Edward close behind.

"Keer wan ar!"

I gazed behind me to the ground in the direction of the voice that broke the silence. I spotted four figures dressed in black armor climbing up after us. Dark Flames!

"Jenna!"

My sister turned to see the Flames and growled. Suddenly an arrow hit a knight in the chest and he tumbled to the ground. I turned to see Edward hook another arrow to his bow.

I turned to Jenna, "Go!"

She transformed into a human, while pulling out her sword leapt over the Flames to the ground. One Flame ran towards her while the other two continued to Edward and me.

Transforming into a human and pulling out the Moon Sword, I slowly charged at another Flame. The demon was covered in black armor from head to toe. A black grizzly cape draped on his back. The demon was a foot taller than me. He slashed his black sword at me while shouting in a language I did not know, but yet I knew the origin, demonic.

I swung back at him and our swords met. I blocked several times before I could get a shot in, only to have my blade blocked by his. As I fought, I noticed Edward in combat with the third Flame. Finally blocking my opponent's sword, I saw an opening and brought my blade into the demon's left side. The Flame screamed in pain and fell to the ground, dead.

I looked to Edward as he brought an arrow into his enemy's shoulder then pushed the demon off the pyramid to the ground, dead. I glanced towards Jenna as she felled her foe with a single swipe of her sword. Edward raised his bow in victory. We both met Jenna on the ground, breathing heavily.

"Where in the blazes did they come from?" asked Edward.

"I don't know, but they were certainly not

frozen," said Jenna.

I sheathed my sword and took a breath, "I don't remember Grandfather's stories having Flames attack here. It was just Cain."

"Agreed," replied Edward strapping his bow to his back.

Jenna looked to the pyramid, "Something is not right. Why would Dark Flames attack us here?"

I shook my head, "Come, we must wait till Cain arrives."

We climbed to a safe spot out of sight and Jenna tapped her watch so time unfroze. After waiting, and waiting, we finally saw Grandfather appear from the entrance. Behind him was Grandmother, and several others.

"You made it," we heard Julie say.

I saw Grandfather hold the gold sword up to her.

"This sword is beautiful."

"And I shall name it Ethril, which means Faith."

"Perfect," said Jocken. "The Sword of Faith."

"Ha-ha, not quite."

Jocken laughed, "True, the real Sword of Faith is sharper than any sword."

Jocken was a big man with huge muscles and a big Blond beard. According to Grandfather's stories, Jocken was full angel like him. It was said he could break the strongest tree with his bare hands. He was also the Delta General. As I looked over the scene I spotted several other people that I had not seen in a longtime. One was **SeeZee**, the colonel. Julie suddenly jumped onto Grandmother's back with apparent delight.

"You're engaged!"

Grandmother laughed, "Yes."

"I remember the story," Jenna whispered to me. "Grandfather proposed in the pyramid right after he found the sword."

Just then the wind picked up as a tornado of sand appeared in front of Grandfather and the others. I wondered if it was my brother, but what I saw made my heart beat faster than a twister. The black armor, the horned helmet, the red eyes, a grizzly black cape. Cain had arrived.

"I have come to be your destroyer!"

I shivered, just hearing that voice made my heart skip a beat. A voice that would make even the bravest soldier cringe. But I was amazed at Grandfather's calmness.

"Remember me, for I am Lord Cain!" With that the demon vanished.

"What do we do, Wolf?" asked Jocken.

"What we've been doing, protecting the world."

After a bit, Grandfather and the others left. Cain appeared again staring off in the direction they went. As I watched him he turned and looked in our direction. I did not know what to think next.

But I felt as if something was happening, and it was happening quickly.

Chapter 8
A Third Vision

I felt myself losing control of my mind. I closed my eyes, a vision appeared. When I opened my eyes, I was on my back on the sand with Jenna sitting near me.

"What happened?" Jenna instantly scooted closer to me.

"Are you alright?"

"Yes, but, what happened?"

"You have been out for almost thirty minutes."

I was stunned.

"Thirty minutes?!"

I tried to sit up but found my head was throbbing in intense pain. No wonder I was so tired, thirty minutes was too long.

"Lay still," said Edward coming to us with his bow. "You must rest."

Where is Cain?"

Jenna looked at Edward then back to me.

"He vanished."

Edward knelt next to me.

"What happened? You just blacked out."

"I...I'm not sure. I saw him. I saw Cain."

"Yes," said Jenna. "We all did."

"No, I mean, I saw his eyes, he looked right at me."

Jenna shivered at those words.

"Do you think he knows?" she asked. "That we're here?"

Edward stood up and walked a few steps.

"I doubt it."

I put my hand on my head to help quiet the pain. I had to think of Jenna's question. What if he did know?

"I hope not. I saw an army in my vision. An army of Flames in black armor."

I heard Jenna gulp.

"Could you tell where it was? The army?" asked Edward.

"A valley, nothing more."

"A valley?" asked Jenna.

I could tell she was trembling.

"I suggest not panicking," said Edward.

"When can we then?" asked Jenna. "I mean, with Ezeryah's visions coming and going like they are, I'm scared."

Edward stared at her then me.

"She has never had visions like this before, Edward."

The archer sighed

"Ok, everyone take a few breaths. As long as we stay together we will be fine."

After a few minutes of clearing my head, I sat up looking at the footprints from Cain. I slowly stood to my feet. I walked to my Grandfathers footprints while turning into a wolf. I smelled the prints as sand covered them from the wind. The scent told me they journeyed, north. I glanced at Cain's prints, seeing they had never moved. I smelled the prints in the sand.

"Should we follow Grandfather?" asked Jenna coming up to me.

"No, not here. We need to go to another time. Another time he and Cain met."

"Yes, we have not seen much here."

I turned to my sister and friend as Jenna glanced at the archer. I knew why she did. I was the one who saw more than them.

"Where should we go next?" she asked turning towards me.

"England," I replied. "The year 1620."

"Is that not the Voyage of the Morning Star?"

"Yes, the year Grandfather sailed to America."

"Well, let us be off."

Chapter 9

England

As I opened my eyes, the first thing I noticed was a small looking town. The next thing was the smells, food! We had appeared between two small buildings that were wooden on the sides with solid white roofs. A dirt road lay in front of us, with a small building for which seemed for food was across the way.

"Anyone else hungry?"

Jenna laughed as she put the watch in her pocket, "Me!"

"I do believe I could do with a meal," replied Edward with a smile.

"Hold on," said Jenna. "Let me start time."

After she did, we walked to the road, looking this way and that we began to cross it. Suddenly a carriage pulled by two horses came charging down the road from the right. I quickly pulled Jenna back as the rig sped by.

"Thanks," she said breathing hard.

"Don't mention it," I smiled. "That wagon was made by a well trained Cartwright."

"Wonder where he was speeding too."

"Don't know, but I don't think they have speeding laws in this time," said Edward.

"I was almost road kill a few seconds ago. They need laws."

We all three laughed.

I turned to them, "I think in this time and others, we should use different names."

"Good idea," Edward smiled. "We do not want anyone knowing who we really are."

"In that case," said Jenna, "We could remove our hoods. If we see Grandfather, I'm sure he would not recognize us."

I nodded as I removed by hood from my head, "Come on, let us, go eat."

Stepping into the building there was a man was behind a counter stirring a giant spoon in a pot of water. As we approached him, he looked up at us.

"May I help you?"

Edward approached with a smile, "Hello, my name...is Frank. Do you serve food here?"

"Sorry, I do not, unless you want dirty clothes to eat. But a ways down the road is an INN. Wonderful food there is."

"Oh, well, thank you kindly."

We walked next door to a larger building made of oak wood. Stepping inside I saw two people, a man with a sword around his waist and a girl dressed in a white dress, a silver sword hung around her waist. The man had a small Blond beard and was dressed in brown leather armor from head to toe. Could it be? It was Alexis, Grandmother's sister, and Gamma Colonel SeeZee. They were at a table, eating. I wrapped my cloak tighter around me as I entered. We slowly walked up to a bar and sat on the chairs. A man came around dressed in bartender clothes.

"What's your fancy?"

"Uh, water?"

"That's it?"

"Well," said Edward, "We are new here. What do you have?"

The bartender lifted a jug of wine to us and took out three small glasses.

"Oh sorry, we don't drink wine," said Jenna holding up an index finger. "Nor any type of brandy."

The bartender looked confused by the words, but he soon poured three glasses of water.

After taking a drink I spoke, "Sir, my name is...Jessica. We are here looking for a ship called the Mayflower."

As the bartender opened his mouth to speak, another voice spoke.

"The Mayflower left yesterday. The Morning Star leaves tomorrow."

I turned to see SeeZee looking at us. I heard Jenna gulp.

"Your names are Jessica and...?"

"Frank," said Edward.

"Mary," said Jenna quickly.

"Pleasure to meet you," said SeeZee. "Warriors?"

I glanced at my sword as the tip of the blade poked out from under my cloak.

"In a way," said Edward. "We are merely travelers seeking new adventures."

"Good to hear. My friends and I are leaving for a new land in the morning. We plan to follow the Mayflower to this new world."

"At least we hope it is," said Alexis.

"True," SeeZee replied. "No one knows for sure what we will find. But my commander is hoping to build a new life for us."

"Commander?" asked Jenna.

"Yes, Commander Wolf is his name. Have you heard of him?"

I shot my companions looks of fear. What to say? Was it wise to say the truth in this matter? I turned back to Edward who winked.

"Yes, we have."

"Where do you hail from?"

"A long way from here," said Jenna.

"Well, you are welcome to come with us," said Alexis. "The Commander built the ship himself."

"It should be an interesting journey with your sister, Amanda, being pregnant," SeeZee turned to her.

My thoughts ran, pregnant? Who could Grandmother be pregnant with? Thoughts raced through my mind as I thought of each of my uncles and aunts. SeeZee picked up a round hat from the table then turned to us.

"The ship leaves tomorrow early in the morning. Meet us at the dock at seven tomorrow."

"We will be there, Colonel."

SeeZee turned to me, "How do you know I'm a colonel?"

I gulped quietly, "Sorry, I just figured you were such."

"Well, no worries, we must be off. Must finish packing."

"Good to meet you both," I smiled.

"I'm sure we will see you around before tomorrow," said Alexis standing from her chair.

"Yes," replied Edward.

As they left, I turned towards to my companions, "Well, we got a ride to America."

The INN Keeper brought us food after a bit. As we ate, my thoughts did roam. A vision of a flock of seagulls over ocean waters as two dolphins play. A ship passing by pushes waves of water to the side. I opened my eyes, how to put that into a story? After we finished eating I walked up to the INN Keeper.

"We need a place to stay tonight."

"Of course, now let me see. Room eight has three beds."

"I will take a room for myself," said Edward from behind me.

"Two rooms, one bed and two beds."

"Of course, room fourteen has one bed as room twenty has two."

"Perfect," I replied.

That evening I stood on a dock overlooking the ocean. The wind was cool and calm. I had my eyes closed as I felt the breeze around me.

"Beautiful night."

I turned to Edward behind me, smiling, "Yes, yes it is."

"The stars are out."

Gazing over the waters, the ocean was still, only moving from a light western breeze, "Tomorrow starts a new adventure."

I felt a hand on my right shoulder, turning back to the archer as he replied, "A new chapter."

"We will see my Grandfather during the journey."

"Where Wolf is, Cain will be also."

I shivered as a cool breeze set in, "I'm nervous."

Edward smiled, "Come, let us get some sleep now. We will need our strength tomorrow."

Chapter 10
Voyage of the Morning Star

That night I had a dream. I was on the back of a large vessel sailing on the ocean. I saw that I was alone. As the waves crashed with each movement of the boat, I heard clanking. I turned to where the helm of the ship sat. Next to the helm was a knight in black armor, then I saw it. Bright red eyes shined from the helmet of the figure.

I felt myself shaking as I spoke, "Cain?"

"He is mine!"

Suddenly the knight lunged at me, I screamed.

† † †

I awoke in my bed at the INN, drenched in sweat. Jenna slept calmly in her bed. All was quiet, except a cricket chirping outside my window. Another nightmare? I shuddered at the memories. I climbed from my bed to the window looking towards the docks. I saw a figure on the dock I had been at earlier. It was dark but I could just make out a cowboy type hat. Was it Grandfather? I was unsure, but one thing was for sure, I would see him in the morning. Climbing back into bed, even though afraid to fall asleep again, I soon did.

† † †

The next morning, I awoke to birds chirping in the trees. I stood looking out my window, I saw an incredible sight. I woke up Jenna and we both came down to the saloon. We saw Edward at a table eating.

"Up early," I said.

Edward turned to see us and smiled.

"My stomach was growling, there was no falling asleep again."

"As is mine," said Jenna laughing.

"Before we continue I have something to show you both, follow me."

We all three came outside looking towards the docks. What we saw was a sight to behold. A great ship sat on the ocean waters just off the docks.

"The Morning Star," said Jenna.

The large vessel had at least ten sails. Three near the front, four in the middle, then three more at the back.

People were everywhere. Several men carried crates onboard the great ship, while others carried their belongings. Dozens of people had gathered to watch the ship leave.

As we stood in amazement, a voice came from behind us, "It is beautiful, isn't it?"

I turned to see Julie, the White Tigress, in human form.

"It is," said Jenna with a smile.

"I can tell by your faces you have not seen anything like this before."

I laughed a bit, "No."

Julie brushed her black hair from her face, "One hundred feet long, three decks, enough room for all. Made out of hickory wood she is, strong enough to withstand almost anything."

"Never have I seen anything so grand," said Jenna.

"You must be the three new arrivals. SeeZee told me of you last night."

"We are."

Edward spoke up, "I am Frank, and this is Jessica and Mary."

Jenna waved as I looked back at the ship.

"When do we cast off?"

"Couple hours," Julie answered. "The crew is getting the last of the cargo onboard. I have a feeling a baby will be born on the trip though."

"What do you mean?" asked Edward.

"My best friend is pregnant, her name be Amanda, wife of Wolf."

Again with Grandmother being pregnant. Who could it be? I still could not remember. I knew my Grandparents had eleven children, but I could never keep track of them all. And two of them were no longer living.

"Well, we shall help however we can," said Jenna.

"No need, I'm sure we will be ready soon. Would you like to meet the others that are coming?"

"Um... sure."

"Don't worry, my commander is very kind."

As we neared the ship I heard a voice, "Welcome."

It was SeeZee. He was dressed nicely in a white shirt and a brown tunic. A brown hood attached to the shirt covered his head. Brown leather pants and brown leather boots with his sword strapped to a belt.

"Morning, sir," said Jenna smiling.

"Well, what do you think?" he asked pointing to the ship.

"It is beautiful," I replied. "Truly the work of a master builder."

SeeZee laughed, "I suppose you could say she has no equal."

† † †

We were soon off. With Grandfather at the front, the Morning Star departed. He was dressed in his usual black armor and long black cape. Soon England was out of sight.

"Do you think we will see Cain during the voyage?" Jenna asked while we watched the country vanish into the horizon.

That was one thing I hoped not, but if we did, we had to be ready. There were dozens of people on the ship, most of whom were Grandfather's soldiers. I was amazed at how calm the ocean's waters were the first couple weeks, but things soon changed.

It was a Monday afternoon. The sun was high in the sky. I sat near the front of the ship when suddenly a shout arose from the back of the vessel.

A minute later, Grandfather, SeeZee, and two other men ran up the steps to the top of the ship near the helm. Every man and woman stopped what they were doing at the sound of the commotion. I saw Grandfather take a spyglass, looking to the southeast. Standing to my feet I looked out over the side to see another ship in the distance. Coming to the helm, I saw Edward talking with SeeZee. He turned to me with a grim face.

"What is it?" I asked him.

He only replied with one word, "Pirates."

Jenna came up behind me just as we heard a shot ring out. Cannons! Looking over the edge of ship, I saw it, a black flag with skull and crossbones.

"We are under attack!" Grandfather cried out. Suddenly, we heard a splash as a cannon ball landed nearby. Every soldier began panicking.

Grandfather turned to the soldier at the helm, "Turn this ship about!"

"Commander," said SeeZee, "we have no cannons ourselves. The enemy must have at least twenty."

"We don't need guns, Colonel. We simply

need to outrun them."

"How?"

Grandfather pointed to the north at several dark clouds, a storm was brewing on the waters.

"We lose them there."

"That is insane," said the soldier at the helm.

"Our only chance," said Grandfather. "Pirates will not rest until they have what they want, by any means necessary."

"Turn the sails to the north!" shouted SeeZee.

Myself, along with several other soldiers, turned the sails so the south winds guided us.

Coming to the ship's deck, I heard Grandfather tell SeeZee, "Make sure she is alright."

SeeZee ran below deck, I knew they were talking of Grandmother.

Slowly but steadily the ship moved north. The pirates gave chase. As we came closer to the storm, I realized we would arrive sooner than expected. The clouds were growing towards us.

"Brave pirates," said Jenna next to me as we watched the enemy ship come closer and closer.

"Or foolish," I replied.

One thing I noticed was the waves were growing as we got closer to the storm. Just then a drop of rain fell on my arm.

"Patch any holes that form," Grandfather ordered. Several soldiers dashed below.

Looking behind us, the pirates were still

coming. I figured these pirates had been through several storms and survived. Could they survive this one? Suddenly a bolt of lightning screeched across the sky as all became dark. Rain poured down as the nose of the ship splashed into the water. The waves were almost as high at the ship. One such crashed into the side of Morning Star causing the ship to turn right. The soldier at the helm did all he could to keep the great vessel on course.

The wind picked up. Julie and Edward pulled on the sail's ropes that became undone. I joined in helping tie it down again. Rain and wind battered my face causing my vision to become blurry. I also found it hard to breathe as the wind grew cooler. I realized the pirates had turned their ship and were firing at us again. Suddenly a huge wave crashed down on the ship sending several of us to the right side wall of the main deck.

"Guns!" shouted Grandfather.

Several soldiers grabbed their weapons and crouched behind the wall of the ship. Shots rang out from a dozen muskets. Glancing over the side of Morning Star, a few pirates were falling into the water as the soldiers continued shooting.

Not knowing how long we would survive this, I gazed to the sky, "Emmanuel, Elohim, please help us."

Suddenly, a large streak of lightning struck down into the main mast of the pirate vessel. The bolt destroyed their flag and split the mast in two. I heard the pirates shouting to retreat.

But then a single voice shouted louder, "All cannons fire on the main sail!"

I glanced over the side again to see a bigger pirate with a red beard and dressed in black and brown leather.

Another wave crashed into us, rocking the boat again. I felt slightly nauseous. Suddenly, a cannon ball struck near the bottom of Morning Star.

Edward knelt next to me, "We must take out their captain."

"How?" I wondered.

"Look!" cried Jenna.

Standing to my feet, I saw it. Behind the pirate ship was a huge wave. The pirates, including the captain, all turned in time to see the wall of water crash down on them. Most of them were swept overboard. But the wave had done more than just take out the enemy. The force of the wave was so great that it tore the remaining masts to shreds.

"Ezeryah, look there," said Edward pointing.

The wave had torn a hole in the ship and water was pouring in. A huge gust of wind pushed at the side sending the ship and her captain over into the sea.

"Turn the ship out of the storm!" Grandfather called out.

I turned to see a ray of sun poke through the clouds to my left. The storm was breaking up.

† † †

About a month in, the day came. While Edward was working with the sailors, Jenna and I had made a project out of a rope we'd found. We had lost our direction in the storm. But with the sun setting, each day, we found west again.

It had been a clear Saturday evening. As the sun set in the west, we heard a great shout. I noticed Grandfather run to the bottom of the vessel. Alexis, Grandmother's sister came up to us with a great smile.

"Sounds like a party is starting," said Jenna.

"My sister, Amanda is in labor."

I glanced at my own sister who returned the look. It was happening. That's when we heard crying, a baby! We all dashed to the lower deck of the ship to find Grandmother crying, as she cuddled an infant in her arms. Grandfather had a leg under her head to keep it up.

He was delighted, "It is a boy!"

"What is the name?" SeeZee inquired.

Grandfather put a hand on the child's head, "A name that means the greatest, Max."

Grandmother smiled, "A perfect name."

I could not believe it, Max! My uncle was the baby to be born. I did not believe how I could have forgotten.

"Uncle Max," I heard Jenna say, "the Silver Wolf."

"The future Silvermoon Sergeant has arrived," I replied.

We both walked up the stairs to the deck of the ship.

"A silver moon."

I turned to Jenna pointing straight up to see a moon as silver as a sword. This was the night, the night that Grandfather's firstborn was to come into the world. Jenna turned to me.

"Are you concerned we have not seen Cain this entire time?"

I thought about the question. It was true we had not seen or heard of the Black Knight since the Pyramids. It had been oddly quiet. And I was alright with that.

"Let us not think on that now, let us enjoy what is happening here and now."

I looked overboard at a dolphin jumping in the air alongside the ship. "I do wish I could swim like one of them."

Jenna smiled, "Laylin can."

I laughed, "True our cousin can become a dolphin, among other animals."

Jenna stretched, "Come, sleep is calling me."

†††

"Land hoe!"

I awoke one bright sunny morning to the sounds of people quickly running about. I came up to the bridge to see small boats being lowered into the water. I spotted Grandfather with the ship's captain near the front of the boat. He was looking at something through a spyglass. I looked over the side of the ship and beyond the waters to see a wonderful sight. Land! After weeks of being sea sick, we had arrived. That's when I saw Jenna helping some of the sailors into the boats. They were going ashore.

"Here at last, young Jessica, our journey ends on the shores of a new world."

I turned to SeeZee looking out over the waters.

"Yes," I replied. "We are here, wherever here is."

I felt a strong hand on my shoulder, "It will be an adventure just finding what's here."

I smiled at him. In all my years of life, SeeZee had become one my best friends. In my time, we did many things together. In the year 2435, we had gone on an adventure together to many countries around the world.

"What do you think we will find there?"

"Care to come along?"

A smile spread on my face, "I would love to."

Jenna, Edward, SeeZee and I got in a boat with a few soldiers as we rowed to shore. At last we reached solid ground. I laughed as Jenna threw sand in the air.

"Sand is soft and smooth here," said Edward feeling the tiny rocks of the beach.

"Seems there is a lot of trees as well," said SeeZee.

I looked at the army of trees inhabiting the land.

"Where do we go from here?"

"I will help the men unload the boat, you three go explore. Report with whatever you find."

We saluted SeeZee then journeyed into the forest. Tall trees some reaching to the sky surrounded us. Grass soon took place of the sand revealing lush greenery. Birds tweeted in trees as squirrels ran from branch to branch. The land seemed to team with wildlife.

"Do you think we will meet any Indians?" asked Jenna behind me.

"Hopefully kind ones if we do," I answered.

We decided to return to the sailors reporting there were a few animals. SeeZee then led us a bit deeper into the land. I knew what to look for, an Indian from History books. We did spot some near a campfire, we decided to depart, leaving them be. We did not want to hurt them, and they probably did not like trespassers. We rowed back to the ship and reported everything to Grandfather.

"We will try another spot," he said.

More land was spotted as we sailed farther South. After landing and exploring a bit, the rest of the soldiers moved to shore. We began cutting trees and building houses. Edward helped Grandfather's army hunt for wildlife, for most of our food was eaten during the voyage.

Chapter 11

A House in Flames

The next year went by slowly, life was hard. We helped and protected as much as possible, while still hiding our identities. Jenna had told us we should build our own house only a hundred yards away from the village. We quickly made friends with some of the Indians, natives of the new world. We had seen no sign of Cain at all. But life was soon to be more complicated then I would have ever thought.

One night in August, we three sat in our home, near a roaring fire cooking dinner.

"Food will be ready in a few minutes," said Edward as he stirred the pot.

I sat in a oak wood rocking chair writing, trying to think of ideas. A cat who made friends with a dog, go on an adventure in the woods far from home. Then my mind went blank. Another idea, a king tries to find a husband for his daughter. The castle is attacked, and the king is killed. A prince saves the princess and brings her to his kingdom.

As I thought of this story, I gazed at Edward. He had saved my life many years ago, from then on I had fallen in love with him, but chose to say nothing of it. He was brave, and had always been loyal and honest, everything needed for a NightFang Captain. I had often wondered if he felt the same about me. But we were soldiers, was there time for love during war? I figured Grandfather had made many sacrifices for Grandmother Amanda even during war, because of love. But was it the same for everyone?

My thoughts were interrupted by Jenna speaking, "You are a great cook Edward."

He turned to her as she sat in a chair reading, "I thank you for such a compliment. When you are as old I am you learn much in cooking."

"I am thirty-two years," my sister replied. "You remember my cake for Aunt Megan's birthday last October?"

"How could I forget? The best thing I ever tasted."

"I still remember the raspberry whipped cream," I said.

"Yes, it did take a while to remove the seeds from my teeth," Edward laughed.

"Still sorry about that," Jenna laughed with him.

A scent hit my nose, "Are you sure it is not burning, I smell smoke."

"Nonsense!" said the archer. "I have kept both eyes on this pot."

Jenna quickly stood to her feet, "I smell

smoke too."

Putting my notebook on a nearby table, I transformed into a wolf following the scent. It came from the window. Getting both front paws up on the sill, I glanced outside. A heavy cloud of smoke was moving in our direction.

"Smoke? Where from?"

"That is the direction of the village is it not?" said Edward behind me.

"You're right of that."

I turned to Jenna picking up her sword, "Should we check it out?"

Edward looked at me with a stare of concern.

I transformed back to a human, "Yes."

After putting the fire out in our own fireplace we gathered our things and ran to the village. Thoughts ran through my mind as to what we would find. I was sure everything was fine. But when we arrived, what we saw what was like a nightmare come true. A house on fire, flames shooting to the sky. People were dashing everywhere throwing water on the fire. I glanced everywhere for Grandfather. I did however notice Edward with a look as if he had seen a ghost.

"Is that not Wolf and Amanda's house?"

I gulped hard. He was right, I felt my heart drop a mile. Jenna was the first running towards the burning house.

I heard a soldier shout near the flames, "Amanda is gone!"

I gazed in fear at Edward who returned the

look. Grandmother, gone? How could this be? We had eaten dinner together with the army, all was fine.

Grandfather came running from the fiery flames, "Max is gone!"

Max? A one year old boy was gone? Edward took his bow and an arrow then nodded at me. We slowly approached SeeZee near Grandfather who was distraught. The Colonel saw us, but no smile came from him. That is when it hit me, Grandmother and Max, were dead. But how could this happen? Grandmother was alive in the future. This had to be the work of Cain. Anger burned inside my chest, Cain was playing with the past.

"SeeZee," I heard Edward. "What happened?"

"I...I don't know. I heard Wolf shout, came out of my house to see this."

"Amanda!"

We turned to Grandmother's sisters running towards us.

SeeZee sighed, "Oh boy."

Edward and SeeZee held the three women back. I turned back to the fire, something was not right. I could sense it.

"Is Gran...I mean Amanda, dead?"

"I don't want to believe it either," said Jenna crying next to me.

"Commander!"

The voice came from behind the house. We all ran to find a soldier who was looking at a tree something seemed to be written in the trunk.

"Commander Wolf," said the soldier. "I think I know who did this."

Grandfather read the carving then turned to us, face pale.

"What is it, sir?" asked Jocken coming from behind.

I read the carvings myself.

"Long live L!"

That was all it said.

"Who is L?" I asked.

"Lucifer," Edward replied.

My heart leaped, the Dark Prince? Hearing that name made my whole body shiver. The sworn enemy of Elohim was responsible for this?

I turned to Edward, "Grandmother is alive in the future. How could she be dead here?"

I could tell he was thinking hard. Just then Daniel the Green Dragon came flying in. Julie was on his back.

"Sir!" cried the White Tiger. "Tracks heading west. Some of which looked as if someone was being dragged away."

"Is it possible they were captured, not dead?" I heard Jocken whisper to Grandfather.

"If that is the case, there is not a moment to lose."

Grandfather soon gathered the army and prepared to leave. Jenna took Edward and I to our house.

"Can you see a vision Ez, of what will happen? A vision of the future."

"What if I see...?"

"You have to try."

I glanced at Edward who nodded. I slowly closed my eyes. A castle, wolves with fur of fire, and Grandfather standing before Cain and a dark figure on a demonic throne. Cain held Max like he was his own. Grandmother was there, a battle began. The vision changed to a forest, Cain running through it. He turns to see the castle in the distance. Growling loudly, he vanishes. The vision changed again. A roaring bonfire with dancing and music with Grandfather along with Grandmother Amanda, the entire army around them, Max sat next to them.

I opened my eyes, Edward was leaning on a tree while Jenna was nowhere to be seen.

"Edward?"

The archer turned to me with a smile, "Jenna! She is awake."

Jenna came out of the house behind me holding her sword, "Anything?"

"A castle, I think where Grandmother and Max are being held. They are rescued, there will be celebrating with music. I believe in the village."

"Did you see Cain?" asked Edward kneeling next to me.

"Yes. He is part of the capturing."

"He captured Grandmother?" asked Jenna.

I noticed my sister clench her fingers around the sword tighter. But I had to think of the question.

"I don't think he was the main part. There

is someone else at work. A battle there will be. But..."

My companions waited. I took a deep breath before continuing.

"I think...Cain escapes."

"Escapes?"

"Grandfather must have defeated him, and he ran."

"Coward," growled Edward.

"So, what do we do?" asked Jenna.

"I feel there is no need to be here any longer. Grandmother and Max survive, though the Black Knight escapes."

Jenna glanced at both Edward and I.

"So, onto another time?"

"We should gather things from the house first," said Edward.

All I could do was nod.

Chapter 12

Legend of Ilandra

After we left America, we had more adventures. This certain adventure I will tell only the important parts. It happened in England, year was 1240. We appeared in a dark forest completely surrounded by trees. I gazed around the night fallen trees as crickets chirped nearby.

Jenna walked up behind me, "Are we in England?"

"Unsure," I shrugged. "What do you think... Edward?"

I spotted Edward near what seemed to be a lake. He was on one knee gazing forward, bow and arrow drawn. I knelt next to him.

"What is it?"

"Voices," he said quietly.

"Where?"

Edward pointed across the lake. A figure stood on the banks of the water.

"Quietly," said Edward motioning me to follow.

I turned to Jenna nodding for her to follow. We silently crept closer to the figure. I could see them, the two red eyes of fire with a black iron helmet, it was Cain. As we hid in nearby bushes, I could hear him talking to himself, but it was no doubt demonic. Just then another voice arose.

"Why do you linger here?"

Cain stayed very still, but spoke, "You know why, my lady."

At that moment, a figure walked out from the trees carrying a bow. A long hooded cape hung over her back. But the voice was not normal, it was almost, undead. The female walked closer to Cain.

"He haunts you, doesn't he?"

"I'm not afraid."

"You don't have to hide your feelings from me."

Cain growled loudly, "I have tried and failed to catch that dog. I am stronger than him!"

As Cain spoke he pounded the ground, which shook beneath us.

The female spoke, "I like it when you get angry."

Cain turned to her.

"I need a fighter that Wolf has never seen. One that will strike fear in his heart."

"I could help with that."

"You want to join me?"

"As lord and lady."

"You still love me?"

"Yes, my lord."

Cain turned to face his friend, "Why? We lead two paths."

"For years we have wanted to fight together. Let this be our time."

Cain laughed, "Your beauty is what makes you evil, Ilandra. But will you keep your promise?"

Ilandra held out a hand to the Black Knight, "Forever."

I heard Edward gulp, "We should not be here. We must leave, now."

"Where?" asked Jenna.

"Anywhere, but here."

We quietly crept away. Suddenly my foot hit a small rock which fell into the water. We all three froze, waiting to see what would happen.

"What was that?" I heard Cain say.

"Hounds, go check it out!"

We heard barking and howling, coming closer.

"Run?" I asked.

Edward turned to me, "Run."

We dashed for the trees, running as fast as we could. I glanced behind me as two creatures chased us. I could not tell what they were but they snarled and snapped like dogs.

"Where do we run to?!" I heard Jenna.

"That building!" Edward called out.

What building? I turned to my left to see a small hut made of wood. We dashed inside with the creatures on our heels. Edward quickly closed the door as The Beasts jumped on the wood trying to break it down. I stood to my feet drawing my sword. Taking a quick look around, I saw there were no windows. Edward held the door shut as it rattled from the force. In the distance, I heard the sound of water bubbling rapidly, no idea what it meant, but we had bigger problems.

"What now?"

I turned to my sister, "Can you freeze them?"

Jenna looked down at her watch around her neck, "I can do that."

"Take my hand!" yelled Edward.

Jenna took his as I put a hand on her shoulder. She carefully worked the watch and clicked the button. Silence, the rattling ceased to nothing.

We waited sixty seconds, nothing.

Catching my breath, the thought lingered, "What do you believe Cain meant by, will you keep your promise?"

Edward nodded, "Asking myself the same thing."

"Do we dare see what's out there?" I asked with a hand over my chest as my heart beat quickly.

"We can't stay here forever," said Edward.

He slowly opened the door, nothing. No beasts or demons.

"Huh?"

"Could they have vanished?" I asked.

"Looks like it," Jenna replied shaking her head.

Edward held up a finger, "Listen."

I transformed into a wolf listening. There it was, the snarling of dogs. But it was quiet. Suddenly a splash of something green like slime hit my nose.

"What the...?"

"What?" Jenna asked seeing the slime.

"Yuck! Slobber."

"Guys!"

I turned to Jenna who was eyeing the roof of the hut. Two yellow eyed demon dogs gazed down at us, not frozen. They both lunged at us, one on Jenna the other on me. The demon on Jenna opened its huge jaws ready to eat. Jenna used her hands to hold the monster's giant fangs away from her face.

Suddenly an arrow hit the dog sending The Beast off my sister. Jenna looked to see Edward hooking another arrow then back to the dog as it grabbed the arrow ripping it from its side. With the arrow in its mouth, the demon bit down on the arrow breaking it in half.

Jenna was instantly to her feet, sword drawn. It was a dog fight between me and the other demon. The hound's brown fur coat was torn and bloodied in several places, these were not normal dogs. One hit across my face left a bad sting on my jaw. We clawed and snapped until my teeth finally found their target on the demon's neck. It fell to the ground dead. I noticed Edward sting the other hound with a second arrow as Jenna ran it through with her blade.

"Everyone alright?" Edward asked looking at us.

I turned into a human feeling my face, "Stinging good."

Jenna took a few small fire leaves from her pocket and sprinkled them on the scratch. After a moment of heat the sting was gone as the scars vanished.

"Thanks for that."

"It is good to do," she replied. "Don't need any venom from a demon's attack taking control of anyone. It's like a bite from a werewolf."

I noticed Edward cringe when Jenna said werewolf. Though I was unsure why.

"Grandfather is able to withstand that," I smiled eyeing at my sister.

"Wolf is an angel," said Edward.

"True," said Jenna sheathing her sword. Looking around she asked, "What now?"

"Anymore demons?"

I gazed around, "Not presently."

"Good, we must go."

"Where?" I asked the archer.

"Back where we saw Cain."

I almost choked on my own saliva, "What?? You can't be serious."

"I am. I got a hunch, must know if it is true."

I gazed at Jenna who tried to show a smile, didn't look like we had a choice.

As we neared the location I looked everywhere for the two demons, they were gone. But to my right was a sight I never wanted to see. Within the trees away from the lake, was a graveyard. It felt like something from a horror film. Demons, undead hounds, graveyards, what was next? I didn't want to know.

"What are we doing here?" asked Jenna.

I could sense she felt the same way I did.

"I'm looking for a tombstone."

"That's a happy thought," I said quietly realizing there were dozens of graves before us.

The archer turned to me, "Anyone got a light?"

I pulled out my sword, waved a hand over both sides while saying, "Wik." (Light)

The moons on the sword glowed, illuminating the darkness. Several tombstones around us lit up with an eerie glow.

"I'm shaking," Jenna whispered to me

Looking around I felt my arm quivering with the sword, "You're not the only one."

We walked the grass around each grave. Several names on them were old and unreadable.

I kept hearing Edward muttering to himself, "Where is it?"

"Edward what are you looking for?"

As he continued he talked, "There is a story, of an undead queen. Ilandra is her name. But it is not her original."

"Did you know her?"

"No, this is 1240, I was born in 1954."

"Good point. Did Grandfather tell you the story?"

"A few times, more then I wanted." Suddenly he stopped, so sudden I bumped into him.

"What is it?"

At that moment I saw his eyes, I was sure he had just seen a ghost. I followed his gaze to a stone with a name I could just make out. Rykell Hedrean came into view as I pointed my sword at the stone. As I looked closer I saw two years. 834-905.

"Whoever this is, she lived a longtime ago from even this time," said Jenna as she knelt to the inscription.

"Ilandra."

I turned to Edward, "What do you mean? Are you saying this is that archer we saw with Cain?"

"Yes, Rykell, as has been stated by Wolf, was a very evil lady who practiced dark magic. People found her out, she was burned at the stake. I fear that demonic archer we saw with Cain, is Rykell."

I was scared out of my mind at that moment.

"A ghost of the past."

Edward drew an arrow.

"We should get out of here."

"Yes, this place is evil," said Jenna.

"Work your watch quickly Jenna," the archer took her hand. "I feel we will be watched, the longer we are here."

As Jenna turned the watches knob, I felt two red eyes already watching us.

Chapter 13

In the Castle of a Giant

More adventures followed. Once we accidently appeared in a field and had to run from a herd of bulls. We found a small town finding out it was 1577 in France.

This adventure however, was different. We appeared in what seemed to be a jungle. Plants that looked like trees. Flowers that stretched to the sky. Rocks that were shaped like mountains. As I looked around I saw another incredible sight. What I saw before me was bigger than anything I could have imagined. A great castle towered into the sky. A set of five stairs that were three times my height led up to two huge wooden doors.

"Where in the world are we?" asked Jenna.

"Everything is so much bigger," I replied.

"A giant."

I turned my head to Edward who was a few yards away.

"Edward, what do you mean, a giant?"

"Look at this."

Jenna and I hurried over to him to see what he was looking at. A giant footprint in the mud lay before us. And we were level with it.

Jenna knelt to the print, "What could have made this?"

"I think whatever lives in that castle."

I glanced at the archer, praying he was not saying what I thought he was.

"Edward, do you mean to tell us...?" Jenna turned to him.

"Yes, I think what lives in that castle is over twenty times taller than us."

After a bit of thinking I thought of what Edward said, "A giant."

Jenna looked her watch over, "Why did the watch bring us here? This is not the time I meant."

"Your watch is working, right?" asked Edward.

"It is."

I looked at my sister, "Nobody panic."

"Any ideas then, before I panic?"

I no idea, I felt like an ant in a huge world. It was all one giant playground, which is probably what an ant thinks of earth.

Edward stood at the steps of the castle, "We could check out the giant's home."

Anyone would think him crazy for saying that, but then the words left my mouth, "Might as well, I'm curious as to what this strange place is."

"How do we get up the steps?" Edward asked.

"You and I cannot fly," Jenna replied standing next to me.

Edward pulled out an arrow and strapped it to his bow, "Anyone got a rope?"

Jenna looked around, "We could use the blades of grass around here."

"Genius," Edward laughed.

Jenna laughed with him.

I walked to a strand of grass which seemed pretty stable, "It would have to be the strongest blade we can find."

"We should only need one," said Jenna.

After a bit of searching we both came back to Edward at the steps with a weed strand. "Perfectly sturdy," I replied.

After Edward tied the weed to the arrow he shot it into the step above us. Jenna climbed up the weed first.

When she was on the next step I called up, "See anything!?"

"No, come on up," she called down over the ledge.

I climbed up next and soon Edward joined us. He took the arrow and the weed and fired it into the next step above us. After what seemed like an hour or more, we finally reached the top. I fell on my back breathing hard.

"My heart beats faster than a racecar," Jenna laughed kneeling next to me.

She extended a hand helping me to my feet. Edward was rolling up the weed strapping it around his quiver.

"Do we have any water left?" asked Jenna.

"A little," I reported handing her my flask.

After a couple drinks, she looked around.

"It's so quiet."

"Too quiet for my liking," said Edward coming to us with the rope around his left shoulder. "And I don't like quiet, period."

I slowly stood up looking at two giant wooden doors before us.

"How do we get in? These doors must be thirty feet tall."

"I don't know," said Edward looking at Jenna. "Need more power then we have to open them."

As my eyes darted back and forth I saw a small crack at the bottom of the door.

"There," I said walking towards it.

As we approached it, I felt around the stones.

"Is it big enough?" asked Jenna.

Edward peered through the hole.

"Looks like a descent size."

"What did you see inside?" I asked.

"Not much, there is a hallway, maybe. It is huge though."

"In that case be extra careful not to get lost," I said with a smile.

Edward winked, "Not in my plans."

"That is a good plan, I like that plan, I think we should keep it," Jenna laughed.

Laughing, I turned to the crack. I put my leg through it, good start. After a small struggle, I squeezed through. I was inside the castle.

What I saw before me was truly an amazing sight. The ceiling stretched up fifty feet. I felt like the size of a pea compared to this place. The walls were ivory with purple and red paint wrapping around pillars from the floor to the ceiling. The floor was a type of smooth white stone. To my left was a long hallway, in front of me was another hallway, to my right was a staircase leading up to door.

"This would take days to explore," I thought to myself.

I turned to Jenna helping Edward through the crack. I had become so mesmerized by the castle I had forgotten about my companions. I helped Edward the rest of the way in. I saw Jenna looking around.

"This place is amazing."

"Agreed, I don't know where to start."

Suddenly we heard the sounds of pounding. As I listened, I realized it was not pounding, it was walking!

Just then a mouse came out of a hole in the corner of a wall. It scurried about the floor seeming to search for food.

"No sudden moves," said Edward quietly drawing an arrow.

As I watched this scene, a vision in my mind clicked.

"Edward, wait."

"What is it?" he asked as I put my hand on his shooting arm.

"Maybe we can use it to our advantage."

"Huh?"

I slowly walked towards the mouse digging in the cracks of the floor. The closer I got, the more it noticed me.

"Ez, what are you doing?" I heard Jenna behind me.

The creature soon locked eyes with me. I slowly drew my sword pointing it at the mouse, which stayed very still, as if watching my every move. I slowly lowered the blade to the stone and removed my hood. I walked over the sword then knelt to my knees extending a hand. The mouse slowly walked up to me sniffing my scent. At first it backed away, then it came again. The mouse had grey fur with a white stripe from its head to nose.

I closed my eyes then tried to speak to the creature through thought, "I will not hurt you. I want to be your friend."

I listened, at first nothing. Then this tiny voice came through, like a squeak.

"Who...are...you?"

I opened my eyes to the mouse nudging my hand. I smiled.

"We are friends, from another world, lost in this one."

"Who are they?"

I turned to my companions.

"My sister, Jenna and friend, Edward."

"Ez? Are you talking to a mouse?" asked Jenna.

I smiled at her, "Yes."

"Of course, you can transfer your thoughts to another. How did I forget that?"

I turned back to the mouse, "Do you know where we are?"

"Athis, you are in the castle of Athis the giant."

So Edward had been right, a giant did live here. I felt panic creep up my legs.

"What did he say?" asked Edward.

"A giant named Athis lives here."

Then something Edward just said boggled my mind, "Are you a boy or girl?"

"Girl," the mouse squeaked.

"Name?"

"No."

"If you will help us, may we ride you?"

"I shall help."

"She will help us, we will need to get around quickly."

"What about us?" asked Jenna. "We have no mounts."

I spoke to the mouse, "Do you know where other mice or creatures might be?"

The mouse seemed to be thinking. She paced along the floor toward her hole in the wall.

She turned to us, "Follow."

I motioned for my companions to do so. We followed the mouse into her hole. It was a perfect little hole, full of comfort. Ok, mostly it was full of pieces of food. But for a mouse, it was home.

"You are quite a food collector," I told the mouse.

The mouse squeaked with delight as if no

one had ever seen her talent.

"This way."

The mouse looked down a space in between the walls.

"You will all three have to ride me."

I turned to her, "May I call you...Marcy?"

The mouse turned to me with what I thought was a smile, "Marcy...at your service, Miss...?"

"Ezeryah."

"Well, Ezeryah, climb aboard."

We all three carefully climbed onto the fur of Marcy, which was incredibly soft.

"Hold on tight."

"She says to hold on."

The others nodded. Marcy took off down the corridors, up and down drain pipes.

"I never thought...I wou...would ride...a mouse," said Jenna bouncing up and down.

She held onto Edward who held onto me as I held onto Marcy's fur. She did not seem to mind the fur grabbing. Finally after a long trek up, we stopped.

"This is where more creatures live."

I scooted off Marcy's back to see another hole in the wall.

Edward stood next to me, "Shall we explore?"

I was getting curious, we had to. Entering through the hole we saw a large room filled with plastic containers and glass jars. Shelves going up to the ceiling towered over us.

"Shall we climb to the top?"

Edward shook his head at me, "Might as well."

He took the arrow and the grass still tied to it and fired it up. After pulling on the grass and seeing it was tight, we began climbing. Marcy climbed quickly up the wooden leg of the shelf. At last we reached the top. What we saw were dozens of bottles and containers stacked on each other. Some big, some small, but everything in this world was huge to us. I walked past a jar and looked in, empty. After looking in several more we concluded this room was empty of creatures.

"Strange," said Marcy. "I could have sworn there was…"

Suddenly something knocked against the glass of a container behind Edward, "I can't tell what it is, Ez, use the light of your sword."

I pointed the glowing sword towards the jar. We were face to face with a creature that had the face and ears of a bat. But as I watched it move about, it seemed to have legs, four to be exact. Then I saw the wings.

"Marcy, what is that thing?"

"I heard the giant and other creatures talking of it. It is a Draat."

"Oh, draats."

I glared at the archer and shook my head, at the same time trying not to laugh at his clever pun.

"What exactly is a Draat?" asked Jenna.

I opened my mouth to speak when, "A dragon bat."

We all looked to Edward, "What do you mean?" I asked.

"The head and fur of a bat, but the body and wings of a dragon."

It all became clear, dra for dragon, at for bat, a Draat.

"Who are you?"

All four of us jumped at the voice. I saw no one. The voice seemed to come from all around us.

"Um, my name is Ezeryah."

"How did you get here?"

I looked to my companions for guidance. Thankfully Edward stepped forward.

"We are lost in this world, we mean no harm to anyone."

Just then I saw a shadow jump overhead, shining my sword to the lid of the Draat's jar, it was a girl, a human. She had long black hair, worn brown pants, a gray long sleeve shirt, and carried a lantern.

"Who are you?" I asked.

"Tira, I serve the giant who lives here."

"You serve him, you are the same size as us. How do you serve a giant?"

"I will not tell strangers like you that."

The girl jumped down revealing her face. I noticed a dagger at her side.

Edward held out a hand, "What if we were friends?"

Tira laughed, "I have no friends."

"Well, believe us when we say, we mean no harm."

"You are warriors."

Tira pointed to our swords.

I smiled, "Oh, yes."

"Where do you come from?"

"Ireland," I replied.

"Never heard of it, is that in Hel-Qar?"

"Is that the land we are in?" asked Jenna.

"Yes."

I noticed Marcy looking afraid, "My friend, what is it?"

"Her."

"Tira?"

"She captures animals and feeds them to the giant."

My eyes grew. Could that be true?

"Do you really capture animals for the giant?" I turned to the girl.

Tira grew an expression of sadness on her face, "I do not. Athis is the one who captures them. He charges me to look after them until he is ready."

"Ready for what?" asked Jenna.

I already knew the answer, to feast.

"How horrible," I shuddered.

"I don't like it myself," said Tira.

"Is that what will become of this Draat?" asked Edward.

Tira looked to the floor, "The giant's supper."

Jenna went up to the Draat's cage.

"What if we were to free it?" I asked Tira.

Tira's eyes grew, "Are you crazy? The giant would have you all for dinner, including me."

I noticed Edward put a hand on the glass of the jar. The Draat tilted its head confused. Edward stepped back laying his sword on the ground while looking at the creature.

"Uh, Edward?" I started, but what I saw next made me stop.

The Draat came closer as Edward put his hand on the glass again. Did it trust him?

Suddenly we heard footsteps, big ones.

"Oh no."

"Tira, what's going on?" I asked.

"Athis is coming, you must all hide. Take your mouse with you. He cannot see her."

"What about him?" asked Jenna.

Tira looked to the Draat with sadness, "I'm sorry."

I looked at the creature who gave me a pleading face. We had to do something. But not yet. We all went behind a pile of jars as a door flung opened. There was the giant. Clothed in brilliant purple and blue robes. A gold crown with red jewels sat on his head. A black mustache and black goatee adorned his face. We watched as Tira faced the giant as he came closer. He was at least fifteen feet taller than us. His voice echoed throughout the room.

"Tira, is the Draat well?"

"Yes, my lord."

"Good, bring him down as soon as possible. Well cooked, all the way through."

"Of course, Athis."

"Remember slave, this better not be worse

then the last one, for your sake."

With that Athis closed the door behind him. We came out of our hiding place to Tira.

"You're a...?"

"Yes," she replied turning to me. "I'm a slave. For twelve years I have done the same thing over and over again. I have watched hundreds of innocent animals die because of Athis."

I felt amazed by the story, "You're the cook?"

"Among other things. The Draat is the last animal in here. Tomorrow Athis will hunt."

"We can't let Athis feast tonight," said Edward.

"Tira, what did Athis mean by, for your sake?" asked Jenna with her hand on the glass jar.

Tira pointed to a jar next to the Draat's.

"The last time he feasted, I accidentally burned the animal. If I do that again, he will eat me."

"Eat you?"

"Yes, Athis is pure evil."

Glancing at Edward, he seemed to catch my thoughts.

"We have to get both of you out of here."

Tira laughed, "Both of us? Good luck with that. I...already tried to escape." Tira showed her left hand, a scar from her wrist to her fingers.

"He promised it would be worse next time."

I gulped, "At least he let you go."

Tira looked to the door of the room, "I can't leave."

Jenna took her scarred hand, "We can help you."

"Why do you want to save me?"

I took her hands, "My grandfather always says, save the life that is meant to be saved. Your life is not meant to be locked in here, it is meant to be free, to be saved. Save the life that is meant to be saved, as my grandfather always says."

Tira looked as if she may cry, "No one has ever said that to me before."

I smiled, "Your welcome."

"How will we get out?"

I glanced to Marcy, "My mouse can get us out of here quickly."

"So can he!"

I turned to Edward who was attempting to remove the lid of the jar. Jenna jumped up driving her sword into the lid. Both used all their strength to pry it off.

"Jen, Edward, get off!" I yelled as I lifted a hand and blasted a wave of force at the jar.

My sister and friend leaped off just in time. There was a snap. Another blast from my hand and the lid flew off. I noticed Tira staring in amazement.

"You are 'powerful' warriors."

We all stood back as the Draat slowly emerged. It seemed to sniff us as it crawled down the side of the jar. Coming to the shelf surface, the Draat seemed to be the same height as us. As I watched, the Draat's head tilted from side to side, it was studying us.

"No one make any sudden moves," said Jenna backing to the edge of the shelf.

"Can't," I said seeing the floor behind me. We were trapped, sandwiched between falling to our deaths, or being ripped apart by a dragon bat.

"Do you think it breathes fire?" my sister asked holding the watch close to her chest.

"I don't," came a voice.

We all jumped back, Marcy had to catch me from falling. Coming to solid surface of the shelf, I stared at the creature, it spoke!

Edward slowly stepped forth, "You speak?"

"Yes, my name is Nylanth."

"Mine is Edward, and we mean you no harm."

"Why would you? A rescue does not mean any harm."

"No, but we could not see that giant eat you."

Nylanth sat on the shelf surface, "You helped me, now I help you. What do you need?"

"A way of escape," replied Jenna.

Nylanth smiled, "Edward, get on my back. The girls can ride the mouse."

"Tira, you can ride with me."

Tira stepped back, "What if we are caught?"

I put a hand on her shoulder, "We won't be, I promise."

Edward carefully climbed onto Nylanth

then helped Tira onto the creatures back.

"We can go back the way we came," said Marcy. "The drainpipes."

I turned to the Draat, "Can you make it through?"

"I can try," Nylanth replied shaking his head.

That's when we heard footsteps, "Athis is coming," said Tira shaking.

"Go go, go!" cried Jenna.

Marcy took off down the shelf leg to the floor towards the hole. I looked back to see Nylanth take flight with his riders holding on. Marcy scurried into the hole as the door of the room opened.

"Tira!" Athis called out. "What's taking so long? Tira?"

Just then Nylanth reached the hole as we heard glass breaking. Athis was looking for us. Marcy took off with the Draat close behind. Up the drains and down some more until we finally reached Marcy's home.

"Take whatever food you want," she told us.

"The castle entrance is near," I told my companions.

"Mouse food?" asked Jenna.

"There must be some kind of human food in here, though it is better than nothing." When our sack was filled I carefully looked out of the hole. No sign of the giant.

"Come on, we have to hurry."

Our mounts took off towards the hole by the front doors. As we reached it we heard a door open behind us.

"Hurry, go, go.”

Jenna carefully slid through the crack, followed by Tira, then Edward. Nylanth had a bit of trouble but was able to sneak through.

“Marcy, this is not big enough for you to fit through.”

“We find another way out, come.”

I could tell my mouse friend wanted to escape.

“Edward,” I called through the crack, “we will find another way for Marcy.”

“Be careful,” I heard him say.

I closed my eyes trying to envision another hole. That's when I felt a breeze. Wind in the castle? How would that be if there was no... window?

A beam of light reflected on my face, looking up I saw a window.

“Marcy, can you get us up there.”

Marcy smiled, “On my back.”

She carefully climbed the stone wall to the window. There was our escape, a hole in the bottom right corner of the glass. Suddenly I heard footsteps, turning, I saw Athis enter the room. He turned looking right at us.

“Get back here!” he roared.

"Go Marcy!”

The mouse scurried out.

I rode her down to the others.

"Go!" I shouted to them, “run!”

Did not have to say that twice. Edward already had the girls on Nylanth as he mounted, the Draat took off. The castle doors burst opened, but Marcy did not stop running. She quickly scurried down the side of the steps to the grass.

As we ran I heard the giant's voice shout, "Release the Beast!"

Release The Beast? What did that mean? We caught up to our companions, who had landed on the ground around some tall grass.

"Edward, I have a bad feeling."

"About what?" he asked stopping.

"I think we are being followed."

Jenna sat on the ground panting, "By what?"

Tira's eyes lit up with fear.

"The Beast!"

I turned to Tira, "What do you mean?"

"A great creature lives within the ground under the castle."

"A great creature?" asked Jenna.

"If Athis has released it, we..."

There was a distant howl and a roar.

"...are in grave danger."

I noticed Marcy and Nylanth cower in fear at the sound.

My eyes darted this way and that all around me. I saw nothing, and heard nothing.

"We need to run."

"Wait," said Edward. "What does it look like exactly?"

"Six feet tall, rows of teeth, brown fur, nasty it is."

"Six feet is not bad," replied Jenna.

"You think so?" asked Edward. "We are the sizes of toothpicks, six feet here is probably one hundred feet tall to us."

Edward was right. The Beast could smash us easily with one pounce. And could probably smell us too. That had to be why Athis released it, to sniff us out.

"Is there a place we can go as to not be found?"

Tira shook her head, "As I said, I have not been out of the castle since I got here, that was years ago."

"If we can find a hole somewhere, we could hide."

"That could work."

"Marcy can you dig a hole?"

"I'm not that fast, though trust me I wish I was."

As I looked around I heard a sound, rustling leaves, sticks breaking, grass cracking. It was coming, fast.

I turned to my friends, "Run, run!"

I kept an eye behind us as Marcy ran. Hopping over rocks and brush I could hear footsteps behind us. Suddenly I heard a scream, as behind me, Jenna had fallen off of Nylanth.

"Jenna!"

"Go!" yelled Edward to the Draat as he jumped off. "I'll get your sister, Ez!"

After running a bit farther I turned to see Edward with Jenna in his arms. That's when I saw a giant hairy leg step down behind them. I looked up to see the face of The Beast. A hairy monster with yellow eyes and long fangs. Its face resembled a saber toothed-tiger. It lunged its huge mouth towards Edward and Jenna. Quickly I jumped off of Marcy, found a rock and threw it as hard as I could, hitting the creature in the face. The Beast quickly reacted to the stone. It turned towards me growling loudly.

Edward finally caught up to us, "We must find shelter!"

I could not help wonder of my sisters safety as Edward ran past.

"Jenna...?"

A voice shouted, "This way!"

We both turned to Tira who was in a pile of leaves. Nylanth was digging quickly along with Marcy.

"A hole!"

Edward darted towards it carrying Jenna, me following close behind. I turned to see The Beast leap into the air towards us. We reached the hole and hurried inside just as the creature landed. The impact sent us all flying in.

† † †

I opened my eyes to see...snow? Where was I? I turned around to see my house. A little ways ahead of me was my father, on the ground. As I walked closer I saw red protruding from his side just inches from his breastplate. He was wounded! Panic crawled up my arms. I rushed to his side as he coughed.

"Father!"

He slowly opened his eyes, "Ez?" He put a hand on my face, "You were right."

"Dad, I will save you."

He smiled, "It is too late. It has happened."

"What? What has happened?"

Father was fading, "I...love...you."

His eyes closed. My heart dropped like a rock. It could not be possible!

"Dad! Dad!"

Chapter 14

The Hole of a Snake

I opened my eyes, head pounding. A small hole of light shined through the darkness I was in. I looked to my left to see Edward, eyes closed, holding Jenna. Tira was to my right, her eyes also closed. Marcy was laying next to me, breathing. Nylanth was at the opposite wall, also out. How long was I out? Where was The Beast? The impact of the creature must have knocked us all unconscious.

The air of this place was foul. I crawled to my sister and put a finger on her wrist. A pulse, I felt relief. More relief when I saw the watch around her neck.

I slowly sat up, another vision, this one felt more real than the others. Had father just died? I shook the dream from my mind, which only made my head hurt.

I looked behind me to see the hole was actually a cave, a tunnel that seemed to go on, but it was pitch black. I stood up trying to clear my mind. I wandered around a few yards looking for something to sit on, finally finding a small rock. After a few minutes Edward stirred. He opened his eyes looking around.

"Morning sleepy head," I said with a giggle.

He turned to me with a smile, "What happened?"

"We were all knocked out I guess."

Edward looked to Jenna and Tira, "They are both out."

"Indeed."

He stood to his feet letting Jenna rest on the dirt, looking to the hole in the ceiling, "How long have you been awake?"

"Not long. This place seems to be a tunnel."

Edward followed my pointing finger to the darkness.

"I have not heard nor seen anything of The Beast."

"Perhaps he is gone."

I sighed, "I hope so."

"We have to get out of this world somehow."

"Not without her."

Edward knelt to Jenna, "She is breathing, thank Elohim."

I walked towards the tunnel, "Where do you suppose it leads?"

"I have no light if that's what you're asking."

"Where is Alezandra when you need her?" I replied. "My sword can only light up so much. I just hope this is not home to something non-friendly."

Just then Tira awoke, "Where are we?"

I knelt next to her, "Cave under the ground."

"Are you alright?" asked Edward as the girl sat up.

"I think so, where is The Beast?"

"Don't know."

"Could he have given up?" I asked.

"Not likely. The Beast wanders until it finds its prey. Do not underestimate him. Athis uses him to hunt"

Nylanth awoke flapping his wings. The archer put a gentle hand on the Draat's head.

"Hold on my friend," said Edward calmly. "Are you alright?"

The Draat stood up shaking its head, "I think so. Where are we?"

"Underground, I guess. Could you scout down that tunnel a bit?"

"Of course."

Nylanth flew up to the ceiling and crawled down the tunnel.

"Well, I guess his wings are alright."

I laughed.

All at once we heard a noise, movement. It seemed to come from the tunnel.

"What is that?"

Whatever it was, was coming closer to us at a quick pace.

"Any ideas?" I asked looking at Tira.

"No, I mean maybe a mole. Or a snake."

I gulped, "Did you just say, snake?"

"Yes, why?"

"I um, have a big fear of snakes."

Edward put his hands in the air.

"Can we not panic, it's probably just Nylanth."

Edward froze in place, sniffing the air, Marcy stood up doing the same. The captain's eyes moved towards me.

"We need to get Jenna up. We are not alone."

Suddenly Nylanth came rushing back to us out of the darkness, "It knows we are here."

"What?" asked Edward.

"A monster."

I rushed to my sister's side and lifted her head to my lap, "Come on, Jen, wake up!"

That's when I heard the hiss. I slowly turned to see a giant snake, its head towering above us. A forked tongue flicked from its mouth, as if sniffing us. Marcy instantly backed away, as did Nylanth.

"Maybe...it's friendly," I quietly suggested, my legs shaking.

Suddenly its head expanded to reveal a cobra, at that moment it lunged. Its brown and black coils shined bright.

"It's not!" Edward called diving away as the snake's face hit the dirt ground.

He quickly moved towards Jenna, carrying her away from the battle. He turned and fired an arrow hitting the snake in the belly. The snake hissed loudly and lunged. Tira and I watched this from a distance. I had to help him, fear or no fear. I quietly drew my sword and jumped on the snake's body plunging my sword in. Green liquid exploded from inside as the snake howled. With one fling of its body I flew to the ground. Getting up dazed, I realized my attack had only distracted the creature for a second as it was still locked on Edward.

"Edward!" I screamed.

The creature lunged at him, it appeared as if it buried him in the ground. But just then Edward appeared on the cobras back. The NightFang was quick. He drew an arrow and fired it into the snakes head. The cobra shrieked then when silent. Its head quickly fell to the ground, dead. As the head landed on the dirt, Edward jumped off landing gracefully on his feet.

"Never challenge a NightFang."

I laughed and raised my sword in victory.

Tira hugged him close, "You saved us!"

Edward laughed as he hugged her back, "It is what I do my lady."

"Ez?"

I turned to Jenna sitting up. She was awake!

"Jenna!"

I rushed to her helping her up.

"What happened? My head is pounding."

"We are in a hole, Miss Jenna," replied Tira. "The Beast vanished."

I turned to the wall of dirt near the hole, "Something is not right, I sense danger."

"I say again, do not panic," said Edward.

I shook my head, "The last time you said

that we were attacked by a cobra."

Suddenly the wall collapsed around the hole as The Beast had dug its way through! I froze in place, hoping not to be noticed. The Beast was mad, it did not seem to see us.

"Oh, come, on!" shouted Tira.

The Beast turned, staring right at us. I gulped.

"Oops," I heard Tira behind me.

I knew she did not mean to give away our position, but now we were in real danger.

Edward scooped up Jenna in his arms, "Down the tunnel, run!"

We ran as fast we could into the darkness, with The Beast close behind. As I ran I drew my sword firing a bolt of light from the blade. The creature stopped for a second as the light scraped its leg. The tunnel seemed to never end. A single tunnel with no light at the end of it. Suddenly it ended, as a wall of dirt blocked our path. Tira screamed causing me to turn seeing The Beast walking slowly towards us. Rows of fangs emerged as the creature roared.

"What now?" I cried.

Edward set Jenna on the ground, "Use your sword. Blind it with the light from the blade."

He quickly shot an arrow which The Beast ducked under sending the arrow over its head.

"You may write that down as the first time I ever missed."

I held the sword tightly in my hand. I closed my eyes as light shot out towards The Beast. The light found its mark, right in the left eye pupil of the monster.

The Beast screamed and roared clawing at it's eye, thinking there was something in it. With The Beast distracted I focused on the next shot. But it was moving this way and that. I could not get a clear shot. Suddenly a hand touched my shoulder causing me to jump.

"Jenna?"

"I shall help you focus."

I turned to The Beast again. I waited for the target. It finally came, my arm was shaking, I could not miss. As Jenna held onto me, the shaking ceased.

"Now Ez!" shouted Edward.

"Wik, Ithai!"

A stream of light shot out from the blade passing between the claws of The Beast into its other eye. The hairy creature roared again, clawing at its face. The Beast continued rolling around blocking our escape. I thought hard, there had to be a way passed.

"I wonder if it would be afraid of a wolf howling," I thought to myself.

I quickly transformed into a white wolf and let out a loud howl.

"What are you doing?" asked Tira as I continued.

Jenna seemed to catch on as she transformed and howled with me. The Beast stopped clawing and backed away from us slowly, still snarling.

I glanced back at Edward who had a smile

spreading on his face. He turned to Tira as he howled, she howled also quietly. The Beast was in panic. All of us howling scared him as he backed away. Suddenly Tira let out a long howl which sent The Beast running as fast as it could to the hole until it was gone.

I transformed into a human falling on my knees, thanking Emmanuel for the victory then hugged Tira close.

"You were brave."

"I was?"

"You scared The Beast!"

Tira smiled. "With your help, we are victorious."

"We won!" cried Jenna.

As we hugged, Edward backed away looking around.

"We must continue our journey in time."

"Yes we must."

"You come with us?" I asked looking at Tira. "You will never be a prisoner again."

"I can?"

"Yes, come with us. See the world."

Tira sat on a nearby rock by the tunnel's wall, "This is the only world I have ever known. Where I lived."

Jenna knelt to her, "There is nothing left for you here."

After a few minutes Tira's face brightened with a great smile, "I'm ready, where do we go?"

I looked to Edward, "Anything?"

Edward sat on the ground in deep thought,

"1862."

"Why then?" asked Jenna.

"There is something you two may not know of," he said to us.

"Like?"

"Your Aunt Kaitlin, was taken by a demon during the civil war."

My sister and I both sat next to him.

"Kaitlin is a fierce warrior, and the demons know that. So, they wanted her to fight with them. One demon, as stated by your grand-father years ago, succeeded. I want to go correct that."

"Yes, Aunt Kaitlin, we will rescue her," I replied.

"There was a battle between the North and the South, during it, Kaitlin was captured."

Tira came up to us, "So, when do we go?"

Jenna held the watch in her hand.

I laughed, "Right now!"

Chapter 15

Civil War

We appeared in a thick forest surrounded by maple trees.

I laughed when I saw Tira with her eyes still closed, "You can open them now."

Tira glanced around, "Incredible. I cannot wait to do that again."

I laughed harder.

"Is this 1862?" asked Edward.

"It should be," Jenna replied. "Better check around just in case."

"Where are we?" asked Tira.

I sniffed the air, "With luck, in the country of America. During a time of civil war."

"Civil war, like two kingdoms fighting each other?"

"Exactly. This was a time of trouble because of slavery."

"More slavery?"

"Not for you, I can assure you. We must find the Union Army. Good guys in the war."

"Do you know what they look like?"

"Like that."

I followed Edward's pointing finger to three soldiers dressed in dark blue uniforms. All three were standing on a nearby dirt road.

"They must be scouts for the army."

"Then I suggest we approach with caution," said Jenna.

"Why caution?"

"Because Tira," said Edward. "They do not know who we are. We must show them we are friends. Leave all weapons here."

We all placed our swords and bow at the feet of our furry companions.

Turning to Nylanth and Marcy I said, "Stay hidden here, we will return."

"Call us if you need us," said Nylanth with a shake of his head.

Edward took a deep breath, "Friends!"

The soldiers turned to the direction of the shout aiming their musket guns at us.

"Who are you?" asked one.

"No need to fear us," Edward continued slowly towards them. The soldiers kept the barrels of their guns locked on us. "We are of the North. We are unarmed."

"You are friends?"

"Yes."

"You don't look of the north," said another soldier, "nor of the south."

Edward looked to me, "It is true. We are of the north, though we don't wear the attire. We are spies."

"We seek an audience with your leader," I

replied.

"Wolf?" the soldiers lowered their muskets.

I stared at Jenna. Did he just say Grandfather?

"Who is she?" a soldier asked.

I turned to Tira and got an idea, "Her house was burned down by Confederate soldiers. She was the only one to survive."

"Is she hurt?"

"She is unharmed. But it is urgent we see your commanders."

The soldiers looked around, "Follow us."

As we walked, I noticed the grass around us appeared as waves as the wind had changed to the North.

"The North wind blows, Edward," I whispered to the archer.

"This Civil War will soon become the Civil Frost War."

I could sense the worry in the archer, "But the soldiers of the North, they are used to snow. It could be an advantage."

"I only hope so. This bloody war was not one of my favorites to read about."

My thoughts turned to Marcy and Nylanth. Hopefully they would be alright. But I knew they would come to our aid if needed.

We arrived at a small camp filled with tents. Union soldiers were everywhere. Some appeared to be wounded, others cleaned their muskets as others sharpened their swords. Most looked exhausted.

The soldiers we followed stopped and

pointed, "Our leaders are probably in their tents. There are uniforms and other things in that green tent over to the left. You may want to change before the battle."

"Here comes Abraham Lincoln now."

Jenna, Edward and I faced the soldiers, "The Abraham Lincoln?"

"Our President," said a soldier.

"Who is this Lincoln?"

The soldiers turned to Tira, "You don't know?"

I stepped in "You will have to excuse our friend, she does not know much about this land."

I knew meeting Abraham Lincoln would be a great honor for each of us.

After the soldiers left, I turned to my friends, "We must look the part. Jenna, take Tira with you. Meet back here in ten minutes."

Edward and I laughed.

After we all departed, I turned to see, Grandfather! He stood outside a tent with... could it be? A long black beard and silk top hat? Abraham Lincoln! The President of the United States of America, during this time.

Noticing a tray with water, I cautiously walked up to them and smiled, "A drink I offer you gentlemen."

"Thank you, kindly," said Abraham.

Grandfather took his drink with a smile. He was dressed in the dark blue uniform of the northern states. It was no surprise when I saw medals on his left chest. He was a captain.

But where was his sword? He did not have it by his side. A sort of cowboy hat, worn by Union soldiers, rested on his head.

"So, Captain, as I was saying the Confederate soldiers will be here by dusk."

"We will have them running quickly, Mr. President."

"Good, I must be off to Lexington. Inform me of anything unusual."

"As you wish."

I watched as Abraham got on his horse and rode away. It was a great honor indeed.

"Are you scared?" a voice asked.

I turned to Grandfather who was looking at me with a smile.

"Well, are you?"

I found my next words hard to say, "I... I fear no evil."

Grandfather knelt down to me, "Well said. You remind me of my daughter, Kaitlin."

"Kaitlin?"

"Oh yes, now may I give you some advice?"
I nodded.

"Don't call her little."

I turned to see Kaitlin helping wounded soldiers. She was kind now, but I knew the stories. 1941, Russia, Kaitlin was face to face with Skeletawn, a demon. She had destroyed his source of power. He then called her little. Skeletawn had soon lost his head, literally.

I shuddered at the thought of a Confederate calling her such a name, it was good she was not fighting. But would that matter? At least I knew where she was. I turned to see Edward emerging from a tent in a Union uniform.

"You look great," I said coming up to him.

He smiled, "A bit tight, but it fits."

"Are you sure you want to do this?"

Edward smiled, "I have a feeling something happened here, and we need to fix it."

Just then Jenna and came out of a tent in a brown skirt with a white apron and white hood. She looked at me shaking her head.

"I have no idea how women wore these."

Edward and I laughed.

Turning to the south I took a deep breath, "The army of the Confederates will arrive soon."

"We got them where we want them," said Edward. "Anyone seen, Kaitlin?"

I gazed around the camp of soldiers again spotting the daughter of the Alpha.

"We must keep an eye on her at all times."

"But it happened during the battle right?" I asked.

The archer nodded, "All the same, we must keep our eyes and ears opened."

"Grandfather is here, we will win."

Jenna came up to my left side, "I saw Kaitlin earlier sharpening her sword."

"I hope the word little is not said to her," Edward whispered to me.

I tried to keep from laughing, "It would be a grave mistake to say that."

"Do you think she will fight?" asked Jenna.

"Most likely," replied Edward. "Wolf was never very good at controlling what she does."

"Watch for heads flying then."

We all three laughed. Tira came out behind Jenna in a white dress with a green apron.

"Perhaps we can help the wounded, Jenna."

She smiled, "I would be honored to assist."

As we walked through the army, I saw a certain soldier sitting on a rock looking to the south.

"Max!"

He looked up at me confused, "Do I know you?"

I stepped back realizing what I said, "Sorry, I mean, can I assist you in anyway?"

Max smiled, "Thank you, I am fine right now. What is your name?"

I thought fast, what was the name I used in England? I figured I would change it.

"Carrie."

"Carrie...?"

"Uh, Carrie Wolf?"

"Really, the same last name as my father's first."

I smiled. Just then a young soldier came up to us.

"Sergeant Max."

"Ah, Eli Scrooge, good to see you."

"Your father would like a word with you."

"Of course, right away. Farewell young Carrie, may our paths cross again someday."

As he walked away I said quietly, "Farewell, Uncle.

†††

The day passed quickly, but soon night fell, the Union soldiers had lined a battlefield. In a forest, across a field, Confederates were emerging from the trees. We had gone back to Nylanth and Marcy watching the southern army approach. I sat with Marcy while Jenna paced, Tira sat on the ground picking at dirt.

"When do we make our advance?" asked Jenna.

Edward stood near a tree looking through the branches.

"Once the battle starts, we look for Kaitlin, and keep an eye on her."

"Then?"

"If anyone tries to capture her, we stop them."

Edward turned to me, "Here," he tossed me a pistol, "Just in case."

I had used a gun, only a few times. I hesitated as I picked it up.

I took a deep breath and said, "This gun will defend."

"Do we know what we are looking for?" Jenna asked.

"Demons can take many forms," I replied.

"Exactly," said Edward, "It is possible our demon could be posing as a soldier of the south."

Guns went off, cannons blasted. The battle had begun. Several bombs landed near us scaring Marcy.

After calming her down I heard Edward, "I see Kaitlin."

I stood next to him seeing Kaitlin crouched near some bushes. She fired round after round. Edward motioned for me to advance to some larger bushes. I took careful aim in the Alpha daughter's direction, waiting for something to try and snag her. Jenna appeared next to me holding something. It was ticking. A ticking time bomb!

"What are you doing?"

"Using time. I can freeze time, run this over to the confederates, try to stop their advance."

I smiled, "Do it."

I gazed back at Kaitlin as Jenna worked her watch. Suddenly a bomb went off near the southern lines, blasting soldiers backwards. I turned to Jenna who was moving the watch in her hands.

"Did you already do it?"

"Where do you think that blast came from?"

I laughed with her. She certainly had time on her side.

Just then Edward knelt next to us, "We need to go in closer."

"Closer?" I asked in surprise.

"Yes, we need a better view of Kaitlin."

"Quietly then, let's move."

We four sat for several minutes in a pile of brush, eyes glued on the Alpha Daughter.

Guns still flared as cannons continued to go off.

I noticed Jenna falling asleep, "Stay awake sis."

"It is getting hard. I can hardly keep my eyes open."

"Eyes closing," said Tira behind us.

Suddenly she fell asleep in the grass. Edward gently nudged her, she was out.

"Almost like a spell took her out," said the archer.

Jenna sat with her watch in her hand her eyes closing again. Suddenly she fell over, I quickly went to her side.

"Is she breathing?" asked Edward.

I checked her pulse, "Yes."

"Good because..." his eyes began closing.

He shook his head, "As I was saying...there is something..." Edward fell over to the ground.

"Edward!"

He was asleep. I quickly took Jenna's watch from her hand and stuffed it in my pocket. What was going on? My companions were falling asleep left and... darkness over took me.

Chapter 16

Morcahn's Castle

A sudden shake startled me from my slumber.

"Ez? Are you alive?"

I turned over to see Edward kneeling over me. I blinked several times while turning my head to see Tira shivering in a corner. Jenna was on my other side kicking what seemed to be a stone wall. I found it weird that no vision had entered my mind, but I was thankful for the break.

"What happened?" I asked.

"Captured, that's what," Jenna growled.

My sister had never liked to be a prisoner of war, or anything.

Edward pointed upwards to the ceiling. A cage like door seemed to seal us in a tall square room.

"Ok, what else happened?"

Edward extended a hand lifting me to my feet.

"We are in a castle of sorts. I awoke for a

few seconds while we were carried..."

I stopped him, "Carried?"

"Sacks my lady, we were carried in sacks. There was barely a peep hole for me to see through. I saw torches on stone walls, then, I heard it."

"What?"

"A name, Morcahn."

"He captured us?"

"My thoughts...he was the one who captured Kaitlin."

"Marcy and Nylanth?" I inquired.

"My guess is they are still in the forest."

Jenna kicked the wall again.

"Ok," said Edward turning to her. "You really need to stop doing that. These are thick enough to keep even the strongest ogre in."

Jenna sighed backing away from the wall, "I hate ogres. The worst thing is the watch is gone."

I could have slapped myself for forgetting, "No it isn't."

I pulled the watch from my pocket and held it out to my sister. Jenna's eyes lit up at once.

"How? How did? What the...?"

"Best way to keep it safe," I smiled.

Jenna hugged me close, "Thank you."

I could tell she was relieved. As we let go, I felt pain shooting down my legs. My head was throbbing, and Tira was crying. Wait...Tira was crying?

"My friend, we will get out of here, no need to fright."

"You...promised."

"Promised?"

"You said I would never be a prisoner again, now I am."

I was taken back. Falling to my knees, I knew she was right. Glancing at Edward and Jenna, I felt at a loss for words. Suddenly I felt weak, as if my powers had been drained. At that moment, I felt completely hopeless, as if the world was going to end.

"We are doomed, the future is lost."

"Don't talk that way," said Tira looking up at me. "Like you said we will escape. We must survive, somehow."

"The future is still in Elohim's hands," said Edward taking hold of me.

"It is over," I cried, the tears came hard.

Suddenly I looked up as I heard Jenna singing.

"A song I sing to you my child, a song you'll want to hear. The road is long the path wide, you dare not along. The moon it shines the wolf it howls, to say you'll be alright."

As she sang I remembered the song, it was Grandfather's Song. He used to sing it to us when we were kids.

As I remembered the words, I found myself singing with my sister, *"You are knight, a warrior, your Faith is all you have. It's from your King, it's from your Lord, to say you'll be alright."*

Jenna sang, *"When you have felt, you are alone, don't dismay I'll come your way, to save you and to protect you, and say you'll be alright."*

I sang, *The lantern burns into the night, the darkness cannot hide. So do not fear, for I'll be near, I say you'll be alright."*

Jenna sang, *"Fear will not win this war, only Faith in our King. He wants to help and protect you, and say you'll be alright."*

I sang, *So wait...wait...the coming day...when you will be...alright."*

I felt tears form down my face as the words of the song faded.

"Grandfather's song," said Jenna kneeling in front of me.

I immediately threw my arms around my sister, crying. It was a moment I would never, ever forget.

"That was beautiful," said Edward behind me.

I looked up at my sister, "Thank you."

Jenna put her hands on my shoulders, "We are not alone in this."

"I do wish I could meet your Grandfather," said Tira.

"You will soon enough," replied Jenna with a wink.

I glanced back at Edward who smiled. We were not alone. Emmanuel and Grandfather were with us. I looked to the ceiling at the bars that held us in. The Moon Wolf was not going be caged as a prisoner.

"Feel around the walls for anything we can use to get out of here."

As my companions searched, I prayed hard. I felt the Spirit come over me, comforting me.

"Found something!"

I opened my eyes as Jenna knelt on the ground near a stone. She knelt down and touched it, it moved!

"You have a keen sense of touch, Time Wolf," said Edward.

She gently pushed again, the stone fell with a quiet thud. Edward pushed on a stone next to it, it too fell.

"How are these so loose?" asked Jenna.

That was a question I had to ponder. Above the cell, I heard someone walking, footsteps seemed to come closer with each step.

"We need to hurry."

My companions carefully pushed each stone next to the other. Soon there was a doorway big enough for us to crawl through. And not a moment too soon.

"Go, go," I quietly urged.

We hurried into a long tunnel that seemed to lead up. We crawled quickly but quietly. There were a few forks in the tunnel. I had to become a wolf to sniff out a right direction. The tunnels were just big enough for each of us to get through. It was mostly dirt with stones hiding in places.

Just then a round room with stones all around as high as we could see was before us. I came out of the tunnel into the room, my shoes grew wet as the floor was water. On the other side of the room were three more tunnels splitting in every direction.

Edward followed in after me, his boots splashing into the water, "Where are we?"

"Lost," said Jenna putting her feet in the water.

As we stopped I listened carefully for any sounds that would tell me we were close, "It cannot be much farther."

"What is?"

"I don't know, a way out, I hope."

"My arms and legs are growing tired," Tira replied coming into the room of water.

I hated to agree with her, but I had to. I could feel my own muscles begging for rest.

"We cannot rest for long," said Edward. "We must get our weapons back."

"And defeat Morcahn before he carries out his plans," said Jenna.

I sat down next to Tira leaning against the stone wall, "If Morcahn was the reason for Kaitlin's vanishing and turn, he must have been smart enough not to call her "little.""

"According to the stories," said Edward, "This was the only time a demon was smart."

"Not if we can change it," I laughed.

"So what do we do?" asked Tira rubbing her legs.

Edward peered down each tunnel, "One has got to lead to stairs."

"And then?"

Edward stared at me, "Working on it," I answered.

Leaning my head back against the stone wall, I turned to the three separate tunnels. I found myself praying. Suddenly something appeared at a tunnel entrance on the far right side. I blinked several times as I focused on the form. A wolf, it was sitting pointing in the direction of the tunnel.

"There!"

Jenna turned about where she was, "What?"

"You don't see it?"

"Should we?" asked Edward gazing in the direction of my eyes.

"A wolf."

Jenna looked again, "Ez, there is nothing there."

"But I see a wolf."

"I too see nothing," said Tira behind me. "Are you alright?"

Just then the wolf turned to me, its eyes glowing...green.

"Grandfather!"

Edward walked to the spot I pointed at, "Nothing."

Jenna slowly walked up to me, "Are you seeing a vision?"

"I...I don't know."

The wolf turned again to the tunnel, then, did it just nod? It did it again. It was nodding towards the dark passage.

"He...it, wants us to go that way."

"Are you sure?" asked Edward.

"Come on!" I yelled running towards the wolf.

"Wait, Ez!"

Jenna turned into a wolf trotting to the right

tunnel and started sniffing, "I smell something."

"What?" asked Edward.

"Fire, and logs."

"A fireplace?"

"Maybe."

She smelled the middle and left tunnels, "The air is foul."

"No thanks," said Tira, "Too much of that in my life."

"Right tunnel it is then," Edward smiled.

My friends caught up to me, we ran down the tunnel until finally, a tall circular room with a winding staircase leading upward. The smell of a fireplace was much stronger here. But so was the sight of a skeleton at the bottom of the steps.

"Who was this do you think?" asked Jenna.

Tira looked as if she may faint or throw up from the sight. I gave her a reassuring hand on the shoulder. Edward crawled looking the bones over.

"My guess, the guy that made the tunnels back there."

"Poor man," Jenna said, "He tried to escape, only to perish here."

I stood to my feet breathing a sigh of relief, "A place to finally plant myself."

Tira gazed up the stairs, "They go on and on."

Is that a door up there?" asked Jenna.

She was right, a small brown door was at the roof of the stairs.

"What would the demon use this for?" asked Tira.

Edward gazed at the door, "Who said we were still under his castle?"

Tira stopped, I could tell she was thinking.

"No way could we have crawled that far Edward."

"It is possible though," I replied rubbing my legs.

I had never felt so sore in my entire life. Crawling on stone had taken all the energy from my knees.

"Are we prepared for what's up there?" Jenna gazed at me.

Edward took the first step, "It's now, or never."

Tira got behind him, then Jenna, then me. We followed the Captain up the stairs. Once we reached the top, my legs hurt so much they could have slid out of their sockets. Edward tapped the door a few times then pushed, nothing.

Jenna turned to me, "Use a vision to see the other side."

I closed my eyes, I focused all my energy on what was above us. I opened my eyes quickly as I had begun to see the red eyes.

"Well?" asked Tira.

"A large room, a fireplace, a purple rug."

"What did the walls look like?" asked Jenna. "A Castle?"

"From what I could tell, yes, stone walls and floor."

"Anything on the door?" asked Edward as he pushed. "Like a lock?"

"No, I never saw it. But I think I can help."

Edward carefully moved aside as I focused a hand through the door feeling for a lock. All I felt was wood for a few minutes, until finally, my hand found it. I pushed the lock until it finally snapped. Edward carefully pushed with me until the door broke free and opened.

I gently lifted the door enough so my eyes were level with the stone floor. There was not much to see, a red couch by a fireplace with a roaring fire, a door at the far end of the room. A long table was by the door, I could just make out something shining from the flames.

Suddenly I felt a force push the door down. The force pushed me down into Edward's arms. It knocked Jenna and Tira down a few steps. There was only a little noise from their fall, Edward held up a finger while holding me. I froze, as did Jen and Tira as they stood up. We heard nothing. Edward let me go as I put my ear to the door. I felt fear crawl up my arms as I turned to my companions.

I said nothing but moved my mouth to say: "He is on the door."

I knew my companions knew who I meant, Morcahn.

Jenna mouthed, "What do we do?" towards me.

I glanced to Edward for help on an answer. I could tell he was speechless. Tira was shaking like a leaf.

What could we do? Standing there thinking, I heard Morcahn leave the door. It was freed. But did we dare open it again? He may have been off the door, but that did not mean he was not in the room. We all took a vote and decided to open the door a crack. Quietly, I opened the door for my eyes to see. Nothing, he was nowhere to be seen. So we opened the door further, till we could see the whole room, Morcahn was nowhere in sight.

Edward got to solid floor first and motioned for us to follow. Quietly tiptoeing to the long table, we saw a beautiful sight.

Our weapons! I gripped the Moon Sword tightly. It was then I heard it, the clapping of hands from behind us. The impeccable sound from someone watching us, now revealing himself, it was a trap.

All four of us spun around to see two orange eyes, a menacing silver helmet with two stripes of black down both sides. An orange and black breastplate with a black falcon in the middle connected to silver and black armored chainmail pants. Morcahn's voice boomed like a giant.

"I'm impressed. You have shown great courage getting this far."

I whispered to Tira, "Get to cover."

Morcahn slowly emerged from his shadowy hiding spot, still clapping his iron hands together.

"Who would have thought, three warriors would intrude on my plans?"

We held our swords at the ready standing our ground. A good thing too as Morcahn drew a long orange blade from a black scabbard.

"So, warriors, it seems the game has ended. Any last words?"

I stepped forward, "May Emmanuel guide our swords."

Morcahn laughed, "Pity, I hoped for something a bit more original."

The demon raised his sword, bringing it down the blade met both mine and Jenna's. The weight of the sword could have crushed a normal human. But we were one fourth angel. We worked to gain momentum. Finally, with all our strength, we pushed his sword away, making the demon stumble backwards. Holding my sword up, I lunged at the demon. Our swords touched, Edward fired arrow after arrow. But even then Morcahn still blocked each one while fighting me. This demon was trained well, but how to match his strength?

I struck several times, only to have each thrust blocked. Jenna joined with me, together we forced him back. We seemed to gain the upper hand, but it was too good to last. Morcahn growled, one swipe of his blade sent us both into a wall.

"Who are you?" asked the knight pointing a sword at my head.

My eyes glared, "I am the Moon Wolf."

Morcahn laughed, "The moon has gone dark, as has your life." The demon raised his sword above me, "No one will ever know of your attempted rescue."

"Demon!"

Morcahn turned to face Edward who had

an arrow poised at him.

"Thank you," Edward smiled.

He let the arrow fly with such speed, it was a blinding light as it rammed through Morcahn's neck.

A high pitch scream echoed through the room as Morcahn fell backwards. I rolled out of the way as the knight landed, dead.

"Edward!" cried Jenna in disbelief, "How the...how did you know to shoot him there? He was covered from head to toe with armor."

"I used the time you fought with him to find his weak spot. There is never armor around the neck. I had to get him to turn towards me, than I saw the spot."

Throwing my arms around the archer I kissed his cheek. I had not taken the time to notice him blush.

"Did we win?" asked Tira coming out of her hiding spot in the corner.

"Yes, we won," said Jenna sword raised in the air.

"Then Kaitlin is safe," I replied.

"True, there is no need to stay here then."

"Can we leave here, like "now?" asked Tira trying to stay as far away from Morcahn's body as possible.

I laughed, "Yes we can."

It took awhile to find the castle entrance but we were on our way to find Nylanth and Marcy. Thankfully the castle was not far from the Civil War battle. We found our friends in the forest, they had not moved.

"Where did you go?" asked Nylanth. "We were about to come find you."

"You did not see what happened?" I asked Marcy.

"No my lady. What happened?"

Could it be possible Morcahn had been far away when we were put to sleep? He must have waited until our companions were not looking, then took us away.

"We were captured," said Edward. "But not to worry, we our victorious."

"Well, that's good news," said the Draat.

"What of the battle?" asked Jenna.

Nylanth pointed his claws to the Northern camp.

"The soldiers of the South retreated. It was quite intense."

That's when I spotted Kaitlin near Grandfather. She was alive, and free.

"Is our job done here?"

I turned to my sister with a slight nod, "Yes."

"Do we go to another time then?" asked Tira.

Glancing to my companions who nodded, she was right. We had come to do one thing, free Kaitlin. We did; now, we could go on with the journey.

Looking to Jenna's watch, I nodded, "Let's go."

Chapter 17
A Face of the Past

"Who are you?"

When I opened my eyes, we were surrounded by five large men dressed in winter white armor. Snowflakes lightly landed on my face.

"Who are you?"

One of them was talking to me.

I took a deep breath, "We are friends. We mean you no harm."

"How did you get here?"

"A good question."

"Where is here?" asked Edward.

"Ahvara," said another knight.

Ahvara, that was a name I had not heard before. I turned toward Jenna who looked scared, and rightfully so, as the knights had swords pointed at us. I gazed right seeing Nylanth being cornered near a group of trees. Marcy had climbed an ice wall out of reach. Tira was on the ground next to Edward, hands up in defense.

"Knights! Make way."

RETURN OF THE BLACK KNIGHT

The men parted as another knight, much taller, came upon us. He wore white plate armor from head to toe with a black and white cape on his back. Thick chainmail gloves gripped a long white sword with a metal tiger head on the end of the handle. This had to be someone of high ranking.

"Please, on your feet."

We all instantly rose. I then saw where we were. A village of ice, and a giant castle loomed before us. Behind us a great brown iron gate stood within a wall of snow blocks.

"I am Captain Lancer. Where do you hail?"

"Uh, Ireland?"

"Never heard of it. Come, perhaps, you should meet the king and queen."

"King and queen?"

"Yes, King Rudolph and Queen Anara."

The knight looked to our furry companions, "Let them free."

The men around Nylanth and Marcy backed away. Marcy quickly scurried down to me. I comforted her as I stroked her ears. Nylanth was a little angry of being cornered and tried to attack the knights, until Edward whistled him over.

I turned to Lancer, "Take us to them."

✝ ✝ ✝

"Welcome friends to Ahvara."

The king sounded kind and gentle. He wore a black and white cape covering thick white armor. A white and gold crown sat on his head. Next to him was a beautiful lady who I supposed was the queen. She had long black hair and a white silk dress with a white crown on her head. I could not speak for I was mesmerized by the throne room.

"Thank you, Sire," I heard Edward say.

"Castle got your tongue?"

I turned to the king who smiled.

"It is beautiful, Sire."

"I made it myself," replied the queen.

"Your highness made this?" asked Jenna.

The queen held out a hand as snow floated up from her fingers, "My name is Anara."

I could tell my companions were filled with as much wonder, as I was.

The king sat on the throne and asked, "What brings you four here?"

"Well, we seem to have come here by accident."

"Accident?" asked Anara.

"Yes, my lady."

"What are your names?" asked the king.

Jenna shot me a glance. To use our real names? I winked at her. Figuring this was a different world, it would be fine to use our real names.

"I am Ezeryah, this is Jenna, Edward, and Tira. And our animal companions, Marcy and Nylanth."

I noticed a look on the king's face as if he was staring right at us, or into us. He rose to his feet and walked towards Edward.

"What did you say your name was?"

"Edward, the NightFang."

"NightFang?"

The king turned to Anara who looked just as puzzled as I was.

"What is it Rudolph?" asked the queen.

"I'm not sure. That name is familiar to me."

At the sound of the name Rudolph I remembered stories Father had told us.

"Our uncle's name was Rudolph."

"It was?"

Jenna stepped forward, "He vanished almost forty years ago, according to the stories. No one has heard from him since."

"Did he?" asked the king sitting on the throne steps.

Silence filled the room.

"It cannot be," I heard him say quietly.

I shook my head, "Are you alright?"

"Yes, but, it is impossible."

"What do you mean?" asked Edward.

The king looked at me and Jenna, "Do you have a father named...Cody?"

I was stunned, how did this man know my father's name?

"We do," Jenna replied, "Why do you ask?"

The king stood to his feet and walked to his throne. He turned to Anara, than faced us.

"Then you have a grandfather named, Wolf."

"How do you know that?" I asked, bewildered.

"Your father, Cody, he is my brother."

I blinked several times trying to figure out if what I had just heard was real. I turned to

Jenna who had wide eyes. Edward looked as if he would choke on his own saliva. Tira just stood there confused by the whole thing.

I took a deep breath, "Your...what?"

"I am your uncle, Rudolph is my name. Alpha Commander Wolf is my father, your grandfather."

"Is it possible?" asked Edward stepping forward. "Are you really the young boy that I fought alongside in the Great Battle?"

That's when it hit me. Edward and Rudolph had been in the Great Battle together four hundred years ago.

"Not young anymore. I am now the Winter King of Ahvara."

Anara turned to him, "Are these your family you have told me about?"

"Yes, but, I have not met these lovely ladies. They were not yet born when I found the portal."

"Portal?" Jenna asked as we all stood.

Rudolph smiled, "You both look just like your mother, Anna."

"How is this possible? You have been here this entire time," said Edward.

"Yes, it is a long story. But what are you doing here?"

"Well, if you're our uncle, then you must have known Cain."

Rudolph instantly stood to his feet, "Four hundred years ago my father knocked him into a hole. What of him?"

Jenna glanced at me then at our uncle, "He

is possibly coming back."

Rudolph sat back down, growling, "How would that even be possible? That hole was endless. Father ran the knight through the chest with the Gold Sword."

"That is kind of what we are trying to figure out. We have been travelling through time finding clues."

The king looked at Anara then back at us.

"How do you think he is coming back?"

"I had a dream," I replied.

"Hmmm, well, I will help however I can."

"Did you see or hear anything that would indicate a return?"

"I did not. I was never near the Great Duel, I stayed with my sister, Kaitlin most of the time."

"You were only twelve at the time of the Great Battle," said Edward. "Wolf and Amanda adopted you only a few years before."

"Yes, they did. You all must be exhausted from your travelling. I shall call for my servants to escort you to your rooms."

✝ ✝ ✝

I opened my eyes to reveal a mountain. I was on a giant ledge looking into a deep hole.

"Could this be Foghorn?" I asked quietly.

As I turned around I saw a great battle scene before me. Dark Flames, even a few NightWolves, soldiers of Grandfather? Dead?

As I walked through the bodies, I felt something behind me. I spun around to see a cloud of smoke spinning in the air like a tornado. As the smoke lifted, a figure clothed in black and silver armor appeared. I felt as if I had seen him before.

Then it hit me, this was the same demon from my vision in WinterFang Forest. I fell to the ground at the sight of him. He pulled out a long silver sword with a black dragon head. I screamed as he raised it above me.

† † †

"Ez, Ez! Wake up!"

I opened my eyes to find myself in a room on a bed. Jenna sat next to me staring.

"Are you alright?"

"Where am I?"

"Uh, Uncle Rudolph's castle."

"Oh right," I thought to myself shaking my head.

I had been so engulfed in the dream I had forgotten where I was.

"I had a dream."

Jenna scooted closer as I sat up, "More like a nightmare, I heard you scream and rushed in here. What happened?"

"I...I think it was Foghorn Mountains."

"What did you see?"

"I...I don't know, a demon."

Chapter 18

Stories of the Past

The next morning we arrived in the throne room, greeted by the king. I had not thought of the dream since I awoke. I didn't want to, I was too scared.

"I trust you all slept well?"

"Yes," said Jenna.

"Come with me, there is something, you must see."

As we followed Uncle down a long flight of snow packed stairs, I whispered something to Edward. At first he gave me a surprised look then nodded as we approached two brown doors. As the king opened them, we beheld an astonishing sight. A large room full of books from floor to ceiling. I had never seen so many in my entire life. Even the most avid reader could take a lifetime to read them all. Where there was wall space I could see the walls were not made of normal stone. Looking closer, they were snow.

"Snow stone," said Uncle Rudolph as he

passed behind me. "Never melts even in the summer."

"This place is incredible," said Jenna. "I have never seen so many books." There must have been thousands of books in this room. Wall to wall, floor to ceiling of books of different sizes, most of which looked dozens of years old. The ceiling stretched five feet above our heads.

Rudolph jingled keys in the lock of a bookcase on the other side of the room.

"I have something to show you all."

The king took a giant scroll from the middle shelf, then closed the door locking it behind him. He undid the strings which held the scroll together.

"What is it?" asked Jenna.

Rudolph carefully opened the scroll laying it across the floor of the cave. What I saw on the scroll cannot all be put into perfect words.

"This scroll is a drawing of my father's entire life until I vanished."

Drawings of Grandfather from his earliest life till the year 2435. Every adventure he'd ever had.

"Incredible," I said quietly.

"Where did you get this?" asked Edward.

"I made it, over the years."

Edward stared at Rudolph.

"You made this?"

"Yes, from the stories I was told through my life."

There were drawings of all kinds, even one of what looked to be two dragons breathing fire at each other.

"What is this of?" asked Jenna.

"What?"

"This picture of someone falling."

Rudolph looked closely at the drawing. He sighed as he pointed to a word with numbers, "What does that say?"

Jenna read aloud, "June 25th 2021."

"The day of the Great Battle," replied Edward.

I looked closer to realize it was Cain falling into the hole.

"The day Grandfather won."

"Yes, that was a day I will never forget."

I looked to my Uncle, "You were there."

"I was. Ten thousand soldiers of Wolf against Four hundred thousand demons of Cain."

"How could Cain return?"

"The answer to that is simple, he is Cain, the right hand of the Dark Prince."

"So you're saying he is coming back?"

"No, I'm saying it's possible. Do you not think it strange Ezeryah, you have a dream of Cain, and then you get told there will be an attack? It is all too perfect."

I looked down at the floor afraid to speak again. The one fear I never wanted to admit was too intense to keep back.

"I just have a feeling he is, all my visions are pointing to the same thing."

"A vision could be of something going to happen, the future. There are many dark forces on earth Ez, all will do what they can to gain control. Anyone could try to bring Cain back..."

"What do you mean, bring Cain back?" Jenna interrupted.

"Cain is second to the Dark Prince."

"But who would try such a thing?"

"Unsure."

"Someone with a power great enough to do so," said Edward.

Edward had not taken his eyes off of a certain spot on the scroll even while he spoke.

"What are you looking at?" I asked curiously.

Edward pointed, "Is this a dragon?"

"Shadow," said my uncle softly. "A fierce beast, known as the Gold Dragon King. Enemy of Dazenth and Julie."

I felt confused by the name spoken.

"Who is Dazenth?" I asked.

Uncle Rudolph went to a shelf at the East wall. He carefully went through each book until he seemed to find what he was looking for.

"This is a book that your Grandfather created years ago, before you were born. Tells of all of us."

He handed it to me opened to a page with a green dragon. As I read through the description, I came to a name of Dazenth. Next to it was the name...

"Daniel, the dragon who killed Shadow?!"

"Yes, his real name is Dazenth, he changed it to protect he and Julie."

"Incredible," said Edward. "I never knew."

"Not many did. But that is a story for another time."

"How did you come by the book though?"

"I copied what he had. It was a way to look back to the real world."

I noticed Jenna looking through the books on the shelf.

"This place is a cave of knowledge. You could spend hours in here."

The king smiled at me, "Written for centuries."

"All of the history of this world," said Jenna looking up. "It goes on for ages."

"Good luck reading it all," Uncle laughed.

"I have time," she winked holding her watch.

"Ha, I'm sure you do."

"We must get back to our world. Is there a way?" I asked.

Uncle stared at me then nodded in sadness, "Not unless you can find another portal. I have tried for a long time to get home. But I am home here now. I can't leave the kingdom."

"There have been no portals since you came?"

"Well, there have been portals, but again, I'm a king. The people of Ahvara are my people now."

"You're right," I replied. "But, we must get back."

"I shall help in any way I can."

I thought for a moment, "Is there a place where portals show up the most?"

The king sat in a chair in deep thought. Finally he stood up and walked to another set of scrolls. He took one out and spread it on a table. He looked at it for a long while. As I glanced it over I realized it was a map of the land.

"Hmmm, the last known report was around here in Misty Rain Forest. That is where I appeared."

"Should we start there?"

"Well it is hard to tell where to start. Portals can show up in random places. This land is huge."

"How long do they stay open?" asked Edward looking at the map.

"That is also random."

"I was afraid you would say that."

"We can start in Misty Rain Forest, we may have luck."

"Let's do that."

The king called out, "Captain Lancer!"

Lancer opened the door to the room, at attention.

"Bring the horses to the gate."

"Yes, Sire."

"Wait."

I turned to Jenna, who was looking at the map.

"How do we know the portal we find will lead us home?" she asked.

I looked to Uncle Rudolph. It was a good question.

"I don't know. Where are you wanting to go in time?"

I glanced at Jenna. To answer or not? There was not much choice.

"2021, Foghorn Mountains."

"The Great Battle?!" asked Rudolph in surprise.

"After it," said Edward. "At least a few days."

"We must visit the place Cain finally fell," I stated.

"Why?"

"A calling, I feel something is calling me to go there. There is something else in that place."

Uncle Rudolph went into deep thought for a bit, "How do you know?"

I took a deep breath, "A vision, last night."

My uncle closed his eyes for awhile. He must have been thinking for he never said a word, which made for an awkward silence.

He finally spoke, "Follow me."

† † †

As we prepared to leave Tira came to us in a barn. I noticed she was wearing maid clothes of winter white.

"Interesting choice for traveling clothes," I laughed.

"Well, the thing is, I'm not going with you."

All five of us looked up at her from our bags.

"You're not?" asked Jenna.

"No, I want to help these people. I actually love it here."

"Are you sure this is what you want to do?" I asked.

"All my life I was a slave to a giant. I'm finally free and have seen more than I ever dreamed, because of you all. I know now there is more out there to explore. And I want to explore more of this world."

I smiled at Tira. In the short time I knew her, she had grown up. She no longer feared, and for the first time ever, she felt at home.

"I'm sure the king and queen would be happy to have you here," said Edward.

Tira smiled, "Thank you, all of you. You saved my life, now I'm indebted to you forever.

"Don't worry about that," I replied. "You are happy now, that's good enough for me."

Lancer came with three beautiful brown horses, "You best be off now."

"Will you come visit?" Tira asked

I turned to my friend and gave her a hug, "Just remember us."

"I'm sure we will see each other again someday," said Jenna mounting her horse.

"Tell your Grandfather hello for me."

As Edward and I mounted, we saluted Tira. She saluted us back. Then we were off with Nylanth and Marcy close behind. We met the king at the gate. His mighty steed was beautifully decorated in snow like armor.

"Heroes, say hello to Delth Carava, which means, White Knight."

"Hello warriors," the horse said.

I jumped, "Did he just speak?"

"I did."

We all three laughed.

"Shall we be off?" asked Edward.

As we rode away from the castle, Jenna asked, "Do you still want to go to Foghorn? We have enough answers."

"There is something more," I replied.

As we rode I glanced around at the land of Ahvara. It was beautiful with its mountains to the Southwest, and forests everywhere else. We came to a thick forest with a frozen stream alongside.

"Welcome to Misty Rain Forest," said the king dismounting.

"Why is it called such?" I asked.

"In the summer, when it rains here, it is mostly a mist."

"You have summer here? Seems it would be winter all year round."

"Ahvara is not like earth. When it is summer it is still cool. Snow can melt, but in the winter, say this was earth. It can drop to minus seventy-five."

"How do you survive?" I asked, dismounting.

"Haha, well, it takes some getting used to for sure. Being king, I have adapted to it. My life is all about winter now."

"Sounds like our mom," said Jenna looking at me.

"This is where you appeared?" asked Edward looking around.

"I remember it as if it were yesterday."

As he walked a bit I heard Uncle say, "Was a day that forever changed my life."

As I watched my uncle, he moved his hand around in the snow as if looking for something. Was he tracking?

"Ah ha!" he exclaimed.

"What is it?" asked Jenna surprised.

"This, my dear niece, is where I appeared."

Jenna dismounted, "Here?"

"This is the very spot."

"How can you be sure?" Edward inquired.

"One thing only few knew about me, I have photographic memory."

"No kidding," I said standing next to him. "In a kingdom as big as this, I would get lost."

"Could there be a portal nearby?" asked Edward walking up behind me.

"I won't say there is. But I won't say there isn't," said the king.

"I hope there is," said Jenna. "I want to be home."

"We all do," I turned to her, "As long as we don't end up on Mars or something."

Jenna laughed.

"I smell nothing but the cold of the air," said Nylanth.

"Sadly portals have no smell," said the king.

"What do portals look like?" asked Edward.

"Purple, blue, or invisible."

I stared at my uncle, "Invisible?"

"Best to keep your eyes opened," he smiled.

I looked this way and that, nothing to be

seen but trees. A portal could be anywhere. I could just make out a frozen lake beyond the forest. I found myself sniffling from the cold wind.

"It will take a miracle for a portal to appear," said Edward.

"Have faith my friend!" Uncle called out ahead of us.

Suddenly, a bright blue flash shown in the east near the frozen lake.

"Portal!" exclaimed Uncle.

Edward stared at me, "Emmanuel is watching over us."

"We just have to hope what we want is on the other side."

Jenna dismounted walking to the giant swirling purple mass, "Are we ready for this? Whatever this might be."

"We don't have much choice," I replied dismounting.

Jenna turned to Uncle, tearing up, hugged him, then walked into the portal disappearing into the light.

"Defend all that is good, Captain."

"You have my word, Rudolph," said Edward.

He gave Uncle a hug then vanished.

As I moved towards the portal, Uncle took my hand, "Ez, remember this, when the road darkens, Faith will be your light home. When sword and shield fail you, the King of kings won't. His fire will never burn out. Don't let the Dark Prince bring you down. Let not your heart fail you."

I felt a tear form below my left eye, "I will never forget you."

The king went to his horse taking a small leather wrapped item from a bag on the saddle.

The king smiled, "Take care of this. For there is much about this land I have not gotten to tell you."

I felt him stuff the item in my backpack, I felt at ease, "I shall protect it with my life."

"Do not let go of hope. For if you do, the Dark Prince will have won. Elohim be with you."

I turned to the portal, taking a deep breath, walked into the swirling mass.

Chapter 19

Separated

I opened my eyes to find myself on my back in an alley. I blinked several times until my eye sight became clear. I slowly stood up while looking at the walls of the two buildings on either side of me. Where was I? Where was Edward and Jenna? Nylanth and Marcy had also vanished. It took a few minutes to realize it was utterly silent. I came to a street to see several cars. But none were moving. I saw a man walking towards me.

I took up my backpack and walked up to him asking, "Where am I?"

But the man did not answer. It took another few seconds to realize this man was not moving. I looked behind him at another man facing the opposite direction. He was not moving either.

I looked above me at the towering buildings. Confused, I continued walking until I arrived at a park. There were frozen people everywhere.

Wait...*frozen?!*

I walked up to a man kneeling in front of a woman. He was holding a box with a ring to the lady who was smiling. The lady had a hand over her heart. I smiled at the scene, wishing that could be me. Walking further, I came to a little girl sitting in some sand by a slide. She held a plastic shovel in her left hand. I saw sand frozen in the air falling from the shovel. Time really was stopped. But how? And where were my companions? I had to find them, and fast.

† † †

Jenna sat up, her head pounding from the apparent fall. She was laying on concrete inside of a large room filled with people. She looked around at all the people and saw a long train in the background. She realized it was a subway. She also realized no one was moving. Did she freeze time on accident? And where was she? She did not mean to come here. This did not look like a mountain.

She reached for her watch around her neck, only to find it was not there. She checked her pockets, nothing. Panic began filling her legs. She did not see Ezeryah or Edward. Fear crept up her arms.

"Keep it together, Jenna," she told herself.

Slowly standing to her feet, she walked around the frozen people. No one moved or blinked. She searched the floor for her watch. What subway could this be? Could someone have picked it up?

No, time was ceased. She came to a man holding a gold pocket watch in his hand. He was looking at it as if to see the time. Jenna carefully looked at the watch and took it in her hands. After looking at it, she saw it was not hers. She carefully put the device back in the man's hand.

She noticed stairs going up and out from the subway. Walking past the people she walked up the stairs to a busy street. A frozen street, as everything and everyone was still. Thousands of people were frozen in step on the streets.

She looked up to see huge buildings stretching up to the sky. Lights and screens on every building. Dozens of cars were halted in time. Jenna looked everywhere on the ground for the watch, nothing.

† † †

Edward awoke with the sun shining brightly in his face. Shaking his head, he looked at his surroundings. All he saw was grey stone underneath him.

He stood up and saw dozens of buildings around him. He went to the edge of the platform he was on, and realized it was not a platform. It was a roof to a twelve story building. He was in the middle of a giant city. But what city? And where were the girls? He then realized it was completely silent. No cars honking, no voices, no nothing.

"Nylanth!" he called out, no answer. That's when he saw a helicopter in the sky, frozen in the air. How would that be possible? He saw a door nearby leading into the building. He carefully opened it and walking inside he saw it was an office. People everywhere were frozen in time. No one moved or blinked. Edward saw a lady at a desk. A coffee cup was tipped over, as the liquid was frozen in the air. The lady seemed to not take notice. Edward carefully made the cup straight. He found a tissue and wiped away the drips from the air. The lady had not moved. Edward walked around the different cubicles.

"Jenna, Ezeryah!"

No answer. No Nylanth or Marcy? Edward unstrapped his bow from his back, he then took an arrow from his quiver. He wanted to be ready for anything. For it was quiet, too quiet.

† † †

The silence continued as I found a bench to sit on, finally, I needed a rest. I was still in the park, no one had moved that I could see. Children were frozen on a nearby swing set. A man was frozen jogging with his dog frozen beside him.

I looked up at a flock of birds frozen in flight. It was all very strange. Whatever city this was, the whole place was at a standstill. I had not seen Edward or Jenna anywhere. I stood up walking to the man and the dog. It was a golden retriever. I gently stroked the dog's fur. That's when I felt it. The feeling I was being watched. I stood up with a hand on my sword, looking in all directions. I walked to the children on the swings. I turned to a young girl walking towards a slide. As I looked at her face, I felt something coming from behind me. I turned to see a knight, a Dark Flame!

"No, not here, not now."

The knight yelled at me in demonic, and charged. I pulled out my sword ready to defend the children. Our swords met, I swiped at him slicing into his left leg. He screamed and lunged at me. I backed up almost into the girl. I had to get this demon away from her. I rolled on the ground passed the knight, he turned and lunged again. Finally I saw an opening and brought my sword into his abdomen. He immediately fell, dead. I sheathed my sword and turned to the children. If the Flames were attacking, how could I defend the people?

† † †

Jenna continued walking through the street. Her eyes glued to the pavement looking for the watch. She came to a restaurant full of people. Stepping inside she kept her eyes on the floor. She almost bumped into a waiter carrying a tray of food, as she was not watching where she was going. She walked around him and kept going.

She saw a watch on a table with a family. She walked up to the table carefully taking the watch. The hands stayed still. Could she make this watch work? She gently turned the knob and listened. Nothing. She breathed on it and listened. Nothing. She shook it, tapped it, still nothing.

She held it in her palm and wrapped her fingers around it tightly, she closed her eyes. She opened her hand and waited, the hands of the watch stayed frozen. She gently put the watch on the table. As she stood thinking of what to do next, there came a sound behind her. She turned to see two Dark Flames moving towards her.

"Really, with all these people around here?"

The Flames seemed to ignore the people and came right for her. Jenna picked up a glass from the table behind her. She threw it at a knight only to have the glass freeze in the air.

"That didn't work."

She carefully moved around the frozen people towards the exit, the Flames followed. Once in the street, Jenna drew her sword, and the Flames charged.

Jenna side stepped sending one over a railing to the subway stairs below. She fought the lone knight until a bad move sent him to the ground, dead. Looking around, she saw no other demons. She realized there were thousands of people frozen all around her. How could she protect each one?

†††

Edward finally reached the bottom of the building to the front door. A man was frozen carrying a briefcase in front of the exit. How to get passed him? He gently pushed the man away from the door just enough for him to pass by. Edward slid past and pushed open the door to sunlight.

A busy street full of frozen people and cars beheld him. As he neared the street, an arrow suddenly shot down in front of him. He jumped back, looked up, seeing two Flame Archers on a building. They were not frozen!

Edward quickly rolled on the ground while stringing an arrow to his bow. Landing to his feet, he fired the arrow into a knight. The last archer rapidly fired arrow after arrow.

Edward jumped in the air dodging each one. While in the air, he fired another shot, hitting the knight in the shoulder. The knight stumbled and fell from the roof to the ground. Breathing hard, Edward thanked Emmanuel for the victory. But something was not right. Flames attacking the city? Edward had to find the girls, and fast!

He had the feeling again, a feeling that was nagging at him for a longtime, he had chosen not to show it. A memory of a battle past, and a girl, love...he pushed the thoughts from his mind.

He had an important mission to complete. Find the girls.

†††

More Flames were attacking in the park! I wrestled the sword away from one and now fought with two swords. A lone Flame was about to slice the statue of a man, I jumped into the air thrusting my new sword into the villain. I came down running the surprised second Flame through with my own blade.

"One more protected."

I had not walked far from the swings so to keep an eye on the children. But I wanted to check on the whole city. It was then I realized, what if Jenna and Edward were not even in this city? What if they were in other parts of the world? Or even, other worlds? I took a deep breath and counted to ten. Feeling more relaxed, I looked around me for signs of danger, nothing.

"Jenna!" I called out. "Edward!"

Nothing, not a sound. It was then I realized I had forgotten about my power. I could attempt to see where my companions were. But what if I saw Cain? I did not want to be haunted by him. But, did I have a choice? I stopped on the sidewalk where I was and slowly closed my eyes. I saw what looked to be a subway and people, I felt a calling there. So feeling this area was safe, I made my way deep into the city, though I still had no idea what city I was in. I came to a street full of people and cars. All was quiet.

I heard a faint sound, and realized I was becoming hungry, so I stopped at a small deli. Walking in, there were a few customers in line. A lady was behind the counter making sandwiches.

It was then I saw a calendar on a far wall, I saw the year. 1995! Certainly not 2021.

Then I saw the sign of the restaurant and a city underneath it. New York City! I was in the biggest city in the world, as I knew, at that time. How was I going to find my sister and Edward in a city like this? And how was I going to get food with time stopped?

A man behind a counter had flipped a hamburger patty into the air. I gently took the meat, seeing it was well cooked. It was tender and incredibly hot. But I was so hungry I took little notice. Before walking out, I put a five dollar bill I'd found on the sidewalk, on the counter. I decided to walk until I found the subway.

Thousands of people were everywhere. I finally saw stairs appearing to lead underground. When I arrived more people and a train met my sight. I looked everywhere for Jenna and Marcy, no avail. I transformed into a wolf sniffing for Jenna's scent. At last I caught it next to a man with a watch just like hers. I tracked it towards more stairs leading outside.

"I will find you, Jenna."

✝ ✝ ✝

RETURN OF THE BLACK KNIGHT

Jenna sat on the ground breathing hard. Four Dark Flames lay dead near her. She looked over at a man sitting next to her. He had a big beard and was not dressed well. She gathered he must be poor for he held out a hat which held a few coins. She dug through her pockets and put a few dollar bills into the hat. The man stayed as he was. If she was going to help the future at all, she would start by helping this man. There was still no sign of the watch. She had been looking in an alley when she was ambushed by the Flames.

She slowly stood and walked to the street, looking this way and that, she saw no sign of demons, just frozen people. She looked up to see a building towering over all the others. Was that the Empire State Building? New York City! She finally knew where she was, but not when.

She continued walking to a library down the road. Entering, there were a few people reading. A mother and daughter were exiting the building, each carrying piles of books in both arms. Jenna sought a way to help. She went to the front counter to see several bags. She took two and brought them back to the people. She took the books from the girl and placed them in one bag then placed the handles on her right arm. She took the books from the mother putting them in the other bag. She placed that bag on her left arm. There, now they both had an extra hand.

She saw a calendar by the front desk. She

saw the year, 1995! How was this possible? Jenna had to find her sister and Edward. She also had to find the watch.

Edward stared at the sky from atop a building, he was waiting for a sound from the girls. Nearby were ten dead Flames, each with an arrow in them. He had walked a long way finding nothing familiar. He jumped off the two story building landing gracefully on a sidewalk.

He walked a ways until he saw a diner. Upon entry, he saw a man and woman at a table. The man had a cup in his hand with a straw which made Edward thirsty. He carefully took the cup and drank the liquid inside. He ended up drinking the whole thing. He set the cup down on the table, then saw a watch on the lady's wrist. He gently took hold of the wrist and saw 1995 on the watch. 1995! How did he get here? He had earlier seen the Empire State Building telling him he was in New York City.

"Is there anyone awake?!" he called out in the building.

No one answered.

"Ezeryah, Jenna, where are you?"

I continued as a wolf following the scent. I

arrived at a fancy restaurant. Walking in I was careful not to bump into anyone. The scent finally ended at a table with a family. A watch was on the table, but I thought nothing of it. A new scent arose which perked up my ears. Foul, demonic. Jenna was here, but she must have been attacked.

Running from the building I saw two black armored bodies on the street. Coming closer, I could see these were Flames, dead. Jenna was on the move, I could sense it. I had to find her. I only hoped the others were with her.

"Emmanuel guide my steps."

I took a deep breath then let out a howl louder then any time before. I hoped that someone would hear it.

† † †

Jenna was still looking around the library when she heard a distant howl. Ezeryah? Having a keen sense of hearing proved great. She rushed to the front door, pushed it open then stood on the steps of the building, listening. The howl grew faint.

"Ez!"

Nothing. She transformed into a wolf and howled.

"Someone please hear that."

† † †

Edward heard a howl. But where from, and

who from? Could it be the girls? He walked in the direction of the howl, hoping the sound would lead him somewhere. He was going deeper into the city. Finally he saw what looked like Times Square. As he crossed the street to the next one, he saw something white to his right. An animal of some kind. As he looked harder, it was not just any animal, it was a wolf!

"Ezeryah!"

The wolf turned to him and transformed into a human with a huge smile.

† † †

I ran towards Edward throwing my arms around him in a hug. At last I had found someone. We were both so happy we spoke at once.

"Where were you?"

"Where was I, where were you?"

"I landed on a building, everyone inside was frozen. Had to fight Dark Flames..."

"Same here, although I was in Central Park. Protecting kids from the demons."

Edward stared at me as if thinking.

"Are you alright?"

He shook his head, "Of course, sorry, just did not think I would see you again."

I smiled at those words.

"Nylanth or Marcy?"

"No, nor have I seen..."

I held up a finger to silence him, I heard a

distant sound.

"What is it?"

"Swords... This way!"

We both ran, weapons drawn, to the source of the sound. We arrived at an alley to see Jenna surrounded by seven Flames, four Flames lay dead on the ground. Edward instantly fired an arrow into a demon sending him to the cement. I jumped into battle to fight two more. Jenna also fought two as Edward fought the remaining. Within minutes the Flames were dead. Jenna had her arms around me at once.

"I thought I would never see you again."

"I'm here now, we are together."

"Not all of us," replied Edward.

"How so?" asked Jenna.

"Notice anyone missing?"

My eyes grew, "Marcy and Nylanth!"

"Oh great, I completely forgot about them," Jenna growled.

"I take it you have not seen them either?"

"Sadly no."

I knelt on the ground resting my legs and thinking, "Is it possible they could be somewhere else in time?"

"What do you mean?" Edward came closer.

"We went through a portal right? What if they are somewhere completely different?"

"Makes sense, your uncle said the portals were unpredictable."

"We will have to hope they will find their way to us somehow."

"Well, in that case now we can get out of

here," said Edward smiling.

"We can't."

I stared at Jenna, "Why?"

"The watch...is gone."

Edward's smile was gone in a flash. I closed my eyes, hoping I did not hear what I did.

"What do you mean?"

"I cannot find it, anywhere."

"Where did you appear?" I asked.

"The Subway."

"We were just there," Edward replied.

"Wait, does this mean you did not stop time?" I asked.

Jenna took a deep breath, "Yes."

I gulped.

"What's wrong?" asked Edward. "You look like you've seen a ghost."

"Cain, it's all coming together. He sent us here, he meant for us to come through that portal. He stopped time."

"Then he is alive."

"I think so."

"Could he have taken the watch?"

"I hope not," said Jenna.

"The watch has to be in the city."

"Agreed," I replied.

Jenna sat on the ground, "What about the Flames? They are attacking everywhere."

"This is a dangerous situation," said Edward.

"One that we will face together."

Edward looked at me with a smile, "You have grown up, a warrior, determined."

I thanked him. He put a hand on my shoulder

looking at Jenna.

"Let's go find that watch."

Jenna slowly stood to her feet looking at us, "I'm in."

"But where to start? A watch in the middle of a huge city will not be easy to find. This is a mighty big haystack."

"And there are watches bound to look like it."

"Could you make another watch work?" asked Edward.

"I already tried."

"Shall we start north, then work our way south?" I inquired.

"It is an idea," said Edward looking on the ground around us.

"Wait, Ez, why not use a vision to see the watch?"

I stared at my sister, she was a genius. But I felt scared.

"I can't."

"Why not?"

"What if I see...him?"

I knew Jenna was aware of who I spoke of, but she was becoming more determined by the minute.

"We do not have much choice."

She was right of that too. Either I try, or we would spend days or even weeks looking. I slowly closed my eyes where I was. After a few minutes I opened them.

"Well?" asked Edward standing next to Jenna.

"Not much to be seen."

"Did you at least see the watch?" asked

Jenna.

"Yes, it is in a dark place. The watch was the only thing I could see."

Jenna shook her head in sadness, "Well, that narrows the possibilities to...zero."

She sat on the steps of a duplex, head in her hands.

Edward turned to me, "Perhaps try it again."

I closed my eyes. After a few more minutes I opened them to feel Edward holding my hand.

"Anything?"

"Maybe a wood floor. But not the watch."

"Not helping," said Jenna looking up.

"I have a feeling this may take awhile," Edward replied.

"It is our best weapon."

I knew Jenna was right yet again. I had to keep trying. I closed my eyes, the image of the watch appeared. I focused on the darkness around it. I did see two red eyes and a black hand reach out at me. I opened my eyes to see Edward pacing.

My heart raced, "Nothing, just Cain."

Edward stopped where he was taking a deep breath, "We know the watch is around wood. What kind of wood? A tree?"

"No, it was almost like, a floor."

"A wooden floor?"

"Yes, but it was very vague. And..."

A vision entered, "A bench."

Edward looked at Jenna, "It is a start."

"Ed, there are dozens of places with wood

floors and benches in this city. We know nothing still."

I nodded, "Perhaps if we move around a bit, I can get more from a different location."

"Not a bad idea sis."

We walked a ways down the road to an intersection. I closed my eyes, only to have the same result. After a bit more walking we arrived near the Subway again.

I closed my eyes, this time, "I saw a door, no, two doors."

"Two doors?" asked Jenna.

"Yes, not sure where to though. But they were clear."

We had stopped at a restaurant to rest. I had used too much energy. Edward had borrowed three glasses of water from another table and three straws.

As I drank, a thought entered my mind, "How do we protect the civilians and find the watch at the same time?"

Edward turned to me with a face of concern, "I don't know."

"Save a life that is meant to be saved," said Jenna taking a drink.

"Every life here is meant to be saved. But how can we save an entire city?"

"Flames are probably attacking the city as we speak," said Edward.

Jenna took another drink and sighed, "Cain really is back."

I turned to her as her eyes faced me, "Yes."

"Why do you want to go to Foghorn still?

We have all the answers."

It was at that moment I heard clanking outside. As I stood up I slowly drew my sword. Edward stood next to me with bow in hand. I raced outside to see twelve Dark Flames attacking statues of people. I instantly jumped into action.

As I fought Jenna continued asking, "Why Foghorn still?"

I was afraid to answer.

"Ez, you can tell me," she said slicing through a demon.

As I cut down my foe I turned to her breathing hard, "Because, there is another."

"Another what?"

I took a deep breath, "Demon."

Jenna narrowed her eyes to the ground then back to me, "Another demon?"

"Yes, there is something we must fix on the mountain. Someone else is coming back to life."

"I'm sorry."

"For what?"

"Pressuring you for an answer."

As I spoke, I felt a presence, spun around knocking the attacking Flame to the ground, "You did no such thing. My visions are everywhere."

"So where do we look for the watch?"

I closed my eyes again. After opening them, I transformed into a wolf snarling and snapping at three Flames, scaring them away from us.

"Well?" asked Edward kneeling to me.

"Grey pots, several of them. They seemed

to be located outside of a building."

"Grey pots?" asked Jenna.

"What building here has such?" I wondered.

Edward seemed to be thinking hard as he paced again.

"There are probably dozens of buildings with pots in this city." Edward looked towards me, "Let us continue walking."

Suddenly a vision hit my mind as I quickly closed my eyes. My head hurt from this one. Opening my eyes, I realized I was trembling.

"What's wrong?" asked Jenna.

I looked this way and that, "Trouble, it's..."

"Calm down," Edward tried to tell me.

Jenna put her hands on my shoulder, "What is it?"

I looked to an alley between two buildings, "There," I pointed.

We ran to the alley to find a terrible sight. A man lay dead on the ground. Jenna knelt next to him checking for a wound. She found it, blood was protruding from his right side.

"What could have happened here?" she asked.

Edward examined the wound and soon looked at us with a grave face, "This man was run through with a sword."

"The Flames!" Jenna cried.

I did not know what to think. I only hoped this was a dream. The Flames were really killing people.

"This city is in danger."

"Ya think?"

I looked to Edward and breathed deep, "Then we must find the watch, now!"

We ran south up one street and down another. All while watching for Flames. No sign of grey pots. At least, not as many as I had seen in one spot.

"Ez, you must try again."

I sat on some stairs leading to a house, shutting my eyes again, I saw more.

"And?" asked Edward when I came to.

"Sky, blue sky, a city down below, I think it was this one."

"I hope so."

"What else did you see?" asked Jenna sitting next to me.

"A needle."

Jenna blinked several times, "Yea not following."

Edward nodded, "We have already established this city is one big haystack."

"And now we have the needle," Jenna grunted.

I shook my head.

"Or at least something shaped like one. It seemed to tower over the other buildings."

"Was it connected to a building?"

"I think so, I could not tell."

Edward began pacing as if waiting for something, or he was thinking. Jenna closed her eyes in deep thought. As I thought hard myself, I glanced up to my right to see a building in the distance. There was something that made me stand and look again. A tower in the shape of a needle sat on the very top of an incredibly tall building. Then everything became clear. That was the building where the watch was!

"Jenna, Edward, I know where the watch is."

The Time Wolf was on her feet in an instant, "Where?" she asked.

I pointed to the building.

"The Empire State Building," said Edward staring in disbelief.

"You have keen vision, sis."

I hugged Jenna, "It took a few tries to see the whole picture."

Edward stepped forward a few yards then turned to us, "Come on."

We all raced to the front of the building, which got bigger as we got closer. We made it to several grey pots in a row with bushes growing out of them, two glass doors in the middle. Hundreds of frozen people and cars everywhere.

"You did it Ez!" Edward exclaimed.

"Come on," said Jenna. "No time to lose."

Actually we had all the time in the world, it was frozen. But with the Flames attacking, I knew what she meant.

Just as we reached the doors, we were ambushed.

Chapter 20

Find the Watch!

Flame Archers appeared everywhere on the street. They fired dozens of arrows towards us. With one wave of my hand a force field surrounded us along with several frozen people. Every arrow bounced off to the ground. The Flames charged. We all three sprang into action.

As we fought I called out to Edward, "NightFang, we don't have time for this."

He nodded while firing arrow after arrow. Five Flames had surrounded my sister. They all attacked her at once. The Time Wolf turned slightly to the left and spun to the right as fast as she could. Within seconds five demons lay dead on the sidewalk. There were still too many, I certainly knew this.

Turning to Jenna I yelled, "Inside! Go, go!"

Running into the building and quickly closing the doors, the Flames pounded on them from the other side, trying to break through.

I put a hand on the doors, transforming them into force fields.

Upon entering the building, there were people frozen, and walls stretching dozens of feet in the air supporting a beautiful brown ceiling with a single large light in the middle. The floor was of a shiny black and brown tile. While the walls were dark brown.

"It could take weeks to search this place," I heard Edward say.

It was true, how could we find a watch in this place? Edward went over to a couple getting their picture taken. He waved a hand in their faces.

"Where do we begin?" he asked looking to me.

"Well, look for a bench."

"Any bench?" asked Jenna.

"I suppose so."

Edward quickly found one, after looking it over, nothing. I too found one nearby, nothing there.

"There must be more."

A thought entered my mind, turning to the doors of the building, I felt around them.

"What are you doing?"

"Something here, this spot."

"Like?"

"These doors, these were the doors from my vision," I looked down at the floor turning as I searched it. "These floors, not wood. Just looked like wood..."

"Wait, wait, wait, "said Edward. "There are

hundreds of floors like this in the building."

I felt the floor with my hand, "These are the ones."

"Then the watch is in this part of the building?" asked Jenna.

"Yes," I replied looking up at her.

She turned around in circles, looking everywhere. Edward walked about the floor, searching carefully.

It was at that moment that Jenna perked up looking in every direction, as if she had heard something.

"Sis, what is it?"

"Quiet, listen."

I listened, nothing. Edward came up to us.

"What's going on?"

Jenna held a finger to his lips. She was silent, listening for something. Her eyes moving in every direction looking for the source.

"There it is again!"

I was feeling quite confused by this point. I didn't like being confused.

"What are you hearing?"

"Tick, tick."

"Like a watch?"

She went to the front doors and stood still.

"I can hear it. I think it's in the wall."

"Your watch is part of the wall?" asked Edward.

"Wait, how can you hear it?" I asked. "Time is frozen."

"Unless it was not the watch that froze time," said Jenna turning to me.

I knew the answer to that, Cain.

"How could you're watch be in the wall?" asked Edward even more confused then I was.

It was then I saw the sun peak into the building. Something on the wall above the doors reflected light at me. I looked at the spot of the glare.

"What's that?" I asked myself.

As I looked harder, I saw three gold looking circles above the doors. One of them seemed to have an object in front of it.

"Jenna? Is that the watch?"

Jenna came to my side looking at the object. She moved closer to it.

"It is!"

Edward instantly used his acrobatic skills and jumped up the wall grabbing the object. He landed perfectly on the floor holding the watch out to Jenna. She took it carefully, her smile grew bigger every second. At last we found it! I had never seen my sister look happier.

"Now we can restore time," I said happily.

Jenna held the watch in front of her and clicked the button. At once people moved, birds in the sky flew with freedom. Time was back!

We all three hugged each other cheering and dancing. People were staring at us with puzzled looks, but I did not care. Looking outside, the Flames had vanished.

"They must have only survived in this world when time was frozen, now it's moving," said

Edward cheering.

I noticed Jenna crying on her knees.

"What is wrong dear sister?"

"I never thought...I would see time move...again."

I laughed while hugging my companions. We had done it. Just then I heard something, my stomach growled.

"My friends, shall we go find something to celebrate with? Food perhaps?"

Jenna smiled, "You read my mind."

We stopped at a small coffee shop down the road. I had to get a strawberry smoothie, as strawberries are my favorite.

As I took a drink I said, "Ah the sweet taste of victory."

We laughed together as we could relax for once.

† † †

That night we made a small campfire in a field outside of the city not far from a forest. The lights of New York came on making the city glow. As Jenna slept, I sat by the fire poking a stick into the flames. I watched as each flame seemed to dance about each other. I was focused hard so on the fire that I did not realize Edward walking towards me.

"Why are you not asleep?"

I jumped at his voice dropping my stick. I turned to him with a smile that quickly faded.

"I'm afraid to close my eyes. I'm afraid I'll

see him again."

"Cain?"

I turned back to the fire and picked up my stick from the ground.

"Every dream from the past week has had him in it."

Edward sat next to me and removed his hood.

"I do not blame you for being scared."

I turned to him, "How do I find courage in fear?"

Edward faced the dancing campfire, "In the One who gives that courage."

I smiled as I knew Who he meant.

"My strength is from Him."

"It is unmatchable strength."

I leaned closer putting my head on his right shoulder, "The Light must break the dark."

I could feel Edward was smiling.

"We are the Light. We are part of this world. Fighting a war against an enemy that is bigger than us. We are soldiers for the King."

"And we believe in our King."

"It is the only way to win this war."

"Fear will not win wars."

"You have grown strong in your years Ez, Cody has taught you well."

"Thank you for being with Jenna and I."

I felt Edward put his arm around me. It was then that I felt something, love.

"As Emmanuel has said, I will never leave you nor forsake you. Nor will I."

I kept my eyes on the flames.

"Do you think we will discover the truth to what is going on?"

"With your determination, yes."

"I feel cold, fear. I'm scared."

Edward let go of me, as I leaned away I saw him unhook his cross necklace from his neck.

He handed it to me saying, "You need it more than I do."

I smiled as he wrapped it around my neck hooking it in place. I took the silver cross in my fingers, staring at it. I glanced back at the archer.

"Thank you."

It was then that a thought appeared in my mind, "If Cain escaped other encounters with Grandfather, what would stop him from escaping the Great Battle?"

Edward looked to the roaring fire. He sighed as he said something I was not expecting to hear.

"I have something to tell you, Moon Wolf."

I turned to him.

"Yes?"

"This is not easy for me to say. Mostly because I'm not sure how. But ever since that night that I saved your life, I have felt something in my heart, towards you."

I felt my heart leap. Was he saying what I thought he was?

"I have felt love towards you. You make me feel happier when we are together."

I took a deep breath.

"You love me?"

Edward turned to me with a wink. My heart leapt higher. For years I had felt love for him. But I had decided not to say anything of it.

"That night that I saved your life, it was because I loved you. I did not want anything to happen to you."

I was at a loss for words as I took another deep breath. Did he really just say...he loved me? Suddenly the words I had kept deep inside, emerged.

"That night, I fell in love with you too."

Edward stared at me. I smiled back. A grin spread on his face.

"Ahem, yes, well, we must find a way back to the future."

"Yes," I replied. "At least we have this time moving again."

Edward smiled, then quickly the smile faded as his eyes narrowed to the fire.

"What is it?" I asked him.

He pointed to the logs.

"Where did the fire go?"

I turned to the now smoking wood. There was no fire, how could this be? The fire had been strong then suddenly, it vanished. I felt a chill like ice creeping up my arms and back. The higher it grew the stronger it seemed. I turned to Jenna sitting up from the grass.

"Why is it so cold?" she asked.

I turned to Edward who held up a finger.

"We are not alone."

I put my hand on my sword as Jenna stood

next to me. Edward quietly took an arrow from his quiver and strung it to his bow. We all stayed quiet and listened. I noticed Jenna reach for her watch.

All at once dozens of Dark Flames jumped out of the shadows. It was an ambush! We instantly attacked. But I quickly realized we were outnumbered.

That's when I heard Edward, "Run!"

We three ran for the cover of the trees. The Flames gave chase. But we were able to outrun them. We stopped to catch our breaths.

"Not good, I feel they are not far behind."

Edward was right, you could not run from them forever.

"You must go."

"What?" asked Jenna.

"You both must go. Continue the quest."

I shook my head, "What about you?"

"Go, I can hold them off here," said Edward.

"But I..."

"Ez, this is your task to fulfill. If you do not find a way, no one will."

I was not ready to leave Edward to fight alone. He had just professed his love towards me, this was too soon. I would not say goodbye. I gave him a look that I was not leaving. He turned to me and gently kissed my cheek.

"Go."

Jenna took my hand, "Come, we have to run. There is not much time."

We ran several yards before I looked back

at **Edward** who had an arrow pointed at **oncoming** Flames. As I closed my eyes, tears **rolled down** my face. The feeling of the wind **rushed past** me as Jenna worked the watch.

Chapter 21

Foghorn Mountains

I opened my eyes as I saw a mist hovering over a giant hole with clouds settling in. Mountains surrounded it on all sides. That's when we heard the wind blow like the sound of a horn. I walked to the edge of the hole and gazed out over the fog.

"Foghorn Mountains," said Jenna behind me. "The location of the Great Battle."

"Grandfather finally defeated Cain here," I replied, my eyes focused on the hole.

Jenna came standing next to me, "No one could survive a hole like this. How would Cain get out?"

The answer to that was simple, he was the Black Knight.

As Jenna walked she suddenly tripped on a hidden rock, falling to the ground. The watch crashed to the ground next to her.

"Are you alright?" I asked rushing to her side.

"I think so."

Standing, Jenna picked up the watch, her face growing more concerned with each passing second. I sensed her fear.

"Alright nobody panic."

Jenna looked to me with panic in her eyes.

"The watch is broken."

I gulped. I was hoping she was joking with me.

"Then you must fix it."

Jenna did everything she could, the watch did not budge.

"Nothing."

"How is that possible, you are the only one who can control it."

"Unless it was a...greater power."

I looked up at her as we both seemed to have the same thought.

"Cain," we said together.

"He has taken the power away. He does not want us to get back to the future."

Jenna growled, "He is doing everything he can to prevent it."

"Can you fix it?" I asked.

"Not easily. I would have to use more power than I ever have."

I put a hand on her shoulder.

"Then hurry, we hopefully have time here in the past."

Jenna clenched the watch in a fist.

"But the future doesn't."

She sat on a rock looking the watch over. Just then I heard clanking. I turned to several

Dark Flames with swords drawn.

I twirled my sword in the air, "I will defend you, Jenna. Just keep working!"

I charged at the Flames directly hitting one in the chest sending him to the ground. I fought with such ferocity several Flames had to attack me cautiously. I felled two more, as I turned to Jenna who was focused on the watch. I saw a knight come up behind her with sword raised. I quickly wrestled a sword from a knight I was fighting and thrust it into the knight behind my sister. He fell to the ground. I continued fighting until the last knight had fallen.

I ran back to Jenna, "Any luck?"

It took me about twenty seconds to realize she had not said anything. I went closer to her. She was very still. I looked at the watch in her hands, her fingers were still as stone.

"Jenna? Are you alright?" I waved a hand in her face, her eyes were still. She did not move a muscle. I put a hand on her right shoulder and shook her gently. She did not react.

"Jen?"

I was getting scared. Was she frozen? It was then I realized, what if Cain had stopped her from fixing the watch? Then I remembered the dream I'd had in the forest, the vision that started this whole adventure. Jenna had come to warn me about the demons. But then she had froze, and I was alone. The dream was coming true, I was alone. She was the only way of getting back to the future. She was the

Timekeeper. Now, we were stuck. This had to be Cain's plan, drive us out of the future. Then he would attack.

I turned to Jenna and gently took the watch from her hands. I looked closely at the dials. I tapped it, shook it, the hands did not move. I put it up to my ear, no sound. I felt trapped and alone, unsure what to do. If Edward was able to get here how could he? He was in a different time, without Jenna. But so was I.

Thoughts ran through my head. What would happen in the future? Would I not get back in time? I shuddered at the thought. I felt a tear coming from my eye. No, don't cry, don't...too late. The tears started coming. I looked over at Jenna. What could I do? I sat next to my sister and leaned my head on her shoulder with a hand on hers. I cried hard, I felt like a failure.

"Elohim, I failed. Jenna is frozen, the watch is dead. The future is doomed. I've failed You."

I noticed light growing on the ground. I gazed up to see a full moon peek from behind the clouds. I looked down at my hands, they were now paws. I was soon a full wolf. But it did not change anything, the tears were still coming. I noticed the light of the moon get brighter on the ground.

Then a thought entered my mind. The moon gave me strength, it could turn me into a wolf. It enhanced my abilities. Could I possibly use the moon to enhance the watch, make it work? I looked at the watch on the ground. I walked to the moonlight staring at the moon then back to the watch. This could work. I stared at the moon and closed my eyes. I then spoke in Angelic.

"Thira re gori-kiv Emmanuel, Thira re miria-kiv re klov (By the power of Emmanuel, by the light of the moon bring power back to the watch)."

I waited, and waited. Tick! I opened my eyes and turned to the watch. The second hand moved as the moonlight made the watch glow. As I watched, the minute hand moved. I looked over at Jenna. Her fingers began moving. Just then her eyes blinked. I smiled as I looked to the moon.

"Gori-kiv Emmanuel (Power of Emmanuel)."

I looked back at Jenna as she shook her head. Since the watch moved, she moved! I trotted up to her as she smiled at me.

"We did it!" I cried. "Now to get back to the future." I walked to the edge of the mountain with eyes closed. "Alright let's go."

I looked back at my sister as she picked up the watch.

"I failed."

I shook my head, "What in the world are you talking about?"

"I was supposed to protect the watch. I'm the Timekeeper. I lose the watch in New York City, then the watch freezes here. I failed."

I looked at the ground and took a deep breath, "No, you did not fail."

"I can't fix the past."

I looked back at her.

"Exactly, it does not matter what happened in the past. What matters is now. What you do now is what matters. Because we have a future in danger. And you are the only one to get us there."

"I feel so..."

"Don't say it, you are not what you say you are."

"Then who am I?"

"My sister, and it does not matter what you did, or didn't do, but what you do now."

"I can't."

It was then I remembered the words of Grandfather's song.

"A song I sing, to you my child. A song you'll want to hear. The road is long the path is wide, you dare not go along. The moon it shines the wolf it howls, to say you'll be alright."

Jenna glanced up at me as I let out a small howl. I could tell she remembered the song.

"You believe I can do it?"

I transformed into a human.

"I always have."

Jenna looked at the watch then me as a smile spread on her face.

"Ok, let's do it."

"No, you won't!" a voice came from behind Jenna.

We both turned to see a figure dressed in

black and silver armor. A silver sword with a black dragon head on the hilt was in his hand. Long black hair and a black goatee. His eyes flashed bright yellow.

I felt immense power coming out from him. This was no ordinary demon. Then a vision entered, this was the same demon from my WinterFang vision, which seemed like an eternity ago. I had told Jenna there was a good reason to come here. But I was perplexed by the visions of him.

"Who are you?" I asked stepping forward.

"I, am Captain Zornoff."

My heart skipped a beat at the sound of that name. Jenna turned to me speechless. I too could not find the words to say. Zornoff was Cain's captain. Then I realized if Zornoff was alive, he could join Cain in attacking the future, we had to defeat him.

"You are Anna's daughters."

My eyes grew, how did he know that? Then I remembered. Three hundred years ago, he kidnapped Mother. According to Father, that's what started the Great Battle. Now we were face to face with my parent's archenemy, and he was alive.

"We are not afraid of you," I said trying to sound brave.

Zornoff laughed, "You are weak."

Grandfather hated that word.

"You are the one who is weak!" shouted Jenna. "You did not survive the Great Battle, you will not now, nor ever."

I had never in all my years heard my sister be so bold. The sound of Zornoff's growl entered my ears.

"We will see who is weak in the end."

Jenna turned to me, "Where is your sword?"

I looked everywhere around me. My sword was gone.

"Not good," I replied.

How was I supposed to fight this guy with no weapon? I could not let Jenna fight him alone. But we had to defeat him. Jenna drew her sword and pointed it at the demon.

"We will fight you no matter what."

"Are you ready to die young one?"

"Are you?"

Zornoff laughed and lunged at her. Jenna jumped into the air landing perfectly on her feet behind the demon. Their swords met with showers of sparks. Jenna held her ground.

I searched for my sword but to no avail. I then remembered the dream. My sword had disappeared. Everything about my dream was coming true. I turned to see Zornoff knock Jenna to the ground and raise his sword above her heart. Suddenly my legs started running towards the demon. My entire body moved with great speed. As he brought the sword down I ran full speed into him. We rolled on the ground. I stood to my feet as Zornoff charged at me. I jumped back as he swung his sword at my chest.

"You cannot defeat me unarmed."

Suddenly a rock hit Zornoff in the back of

the head. He turned to see Jenna holding another rock in her hand.

"You have both of us to worry about."

Zornoff laughed, "Your sister is defenseless, and you cannot match my power. How do I have both of you to worry about?"

"Because of this."

Zornoff turned to me, eyes widening. I had transformed into a wolf. Zornoff turned again as Jenna charged at him, their swords met. I saw my chance and jumped on the demon trying to bite his right arm. He flipped me off his back to the ground. Zornoff finally knocked Jenna's sword from her hands as she went to the ground again. I charged at him snarling and snapping. Zornoff swung his blade. I ducked then bit at his leg. Zornoff screamed from the pain. He shook his leg, pulsating me to the ground. He turned to me angry.

"You will be the first to know death."

I tried to stand, but my left leg was in a world of pain. Fear was returning, I was afraid. I knew death was soon to come. As Zornoff raised his sword above me, an arrow suddenly hit his back. Zornoff turned to the source of the arrow. I stretched to see Edward. Wait...Edward! He had saved my life a second time. He had another arrow strapped to his bow ready to shoot again.

"Leave her be."

Zornoff laughed, "You are brave NightWolf."

"Three hundred years ago Cody sent you off a cliff. I watched it happen. You killed Anna's brother. And by the way, I'm a NightFang."

Zornoff took a step closer, "Changed your ways have we?"

Edward was not backing down.

"Prepare to fall again demon."

"I will never be gone!"

"You will be."

They charged each other. Zornoff swung his sword madly while Edward swung his bow firing arrows when able. I changed back to a human as I struggled to stand, my legs trembled and arms ached. That's when I closed my eyes and prayed quietly.

"My King, help me, I feel weak. We need Your help, Lord."

"Ezeryah."

I heard the voice, not knowing where it came from.

"Ezeryah, get up, keep fighting."

I looked up to see a figure standing over me wearing white armor from head to toe. He was huge, possibly nine foot. A sword of diamond hung on his waist. He was like a ghost. The great knight knelt next to me and offered a hand.

"Who are you?" I asked.

It was then I saw a gold crown with twelve jewels, each different colors, within the gold. It sat on a white iron looking helmet which covered the man's face.

"Emmanuel?"

"Take My hand, I am with you. Believe in that which is unseen. Fight."

The voice was kind, gentle, and loving. I put my hand in His as He lifted me up. At that moment, I felt strength and warmth. I closed my eyes again, when I opened them I was on my knees. It was another vision. But this one, had the Son of Elohim. He was with me. I could do this.

"Faith, must have Faith."

At that moment a sword appeared on the rocks next to me. It was the Moon Sword! I picked up my sword, gripping it tightly while walking slowly to Zornoff who had knocked Edward to the ground. I stopped next to Jenna who was knocked out by a pile of rocks, then turned to the demon. The arrow did not seem to slow him down.

"Zornoff!"

The demon turned to me growling. He soon roared with laughter as he saw me struggling to keep my balance.

"Still trying to be the hero?"

"I am the hero. I am the Moon Wolf."

Zornoff roared again with laughter, "Can you protect your King's people?"

"I am a defender of Emmanuel's flock."

"Fire will consume it. You are writing your death sentence! You know this right? Are you really willing to die for nothing?!"

I held my sword in front of me, I had to overcome this demon, no matter what. Even if I had to give my own life. It was at that moment, I felt a new strength come over me.

"Darkness will destroy the light!"

I growled, "I am the light that beats the dark."

"Perhaps you should retreat."

Retreat? Father always taught us to never retreat, because we were of the King. I growled at the demon.

"Wolves never retreat. We never accept defeat. We are a Fire of Elohim, and forever we will be."

"As you wish. Prepare to die, fool!"

Zornoff swung his sword at my head. I ducked and swiped at his legs. He jumped and brought his sword down towards my head. I raised my sword blocking his. He swung again, sword raised I blocked again, and again, while advancing my strikes. Zornoff started retreating slowly.

I swung the sword with all my strength. The impact on his blade sent it flying several yards away. Zornoff lunged at me. I side stepped and brought my sword into his side. He froze in place, glancing down at the blade, as I withdrew. I noticed Edward standing to his feet holding his bow.

Zornoff stumbled backwards, glancing at me with a stunned face. He growled and raising his hands towards me lunged at me. I side stepped again, he tripped on a rock and fell to the rocks below. Jenna came over to me as I fell to my knees breathing hard.

"Ez, how did you...?"

"It was...Emmanuel, He was with me."

She smiled as Edward knelt next to me. I

instantly threw my arms around him.

"How did you get here?"

"That is not important. Right now we need to get home. 2375 is waiting for us."

I turned to Jenna who smiled. Walking to the edge of the mountain, we closed our eyes as Jenna turned the knob on the watch.

As air swirled around us, I grew concerned about what would be waiting for us in the future.

Chapter 22

The Battle of WinterFang Forest

As told to me by my father, Captain Cody, & my mother, Anna

Father arrived in the Moon Den where Delthar and Zander were looking at a map of land around our house.

"Anyone seen Jenna, or Ezeryah?"

Zander looked up at him, "No, nor have I seen Edward. We are still figuring out how the horses got out of the stables."

"I feel something is coming, and quickly," said Delthar who was already in dark green battle armor of the NightWolves.

Father bent over the map looking at the house.

"No matter what happens, keep the fight away from here."

"Where then?"

"The forest. Whatever is coming must not reach here."

"We must summon the NightFangs. Disperse

some around the house," said Zander.

"More NightGuards then Fangs," replied Father.

Father took several small metal bows and arrows from a wooden box he had brought in. He laid each one out in a row across the map. These were like toys, the children of Ahntharo Village play with them often. But Father used them for battle planning.

There were five different pieces, each one representing a Soldier of the Moon. A bow and arrow for the NightFangs, a long sword for the NightGuards, a double bladed sword for the NightWolves, a rapier for the Night-Blades, and two daggers making a cross shape for the NightHunters.

"Two rows of NightFangs," he said. Then he took several double bladed swords and scattered them in a line in from the bows and arrows. "One row of NightWolves." He took the rapiers and spread them within the double bladed swords. "One row of NightBlades. The NightHunters will be in the back. The Fangs will fire first. When I give the charge, the Wolves and Blades will attack. The Hunters will be last to charge."

"And the NightGuards will be...?" asked Zander.

"Around the house, in case any demon makes it passed us. Captain, get your men into position."

Zander saluted him, "I will start that at once."

As the captain left, Father turned to Delthar.

"We do not have much..."

Katie entered the room. Delthar offered a slight bow. Father took her hands in his.

"Ah, Princess, just who I wanted to see. Are the WolfDragons ready?"

"Yes, Father."

"Good, be prepared to get them in the air."

Just then a NightFang ran into the room.

"Sir, NightHunters have spotted an army seen in the west."

"Glenarm is in the west," said Katie. "What did it look like?"

"Reports are of an army of Dark Flame."

Father narrowed his eyes to Delthar with a concerned look.

"Dark Flames? Is that not what Ezeryah was saying yesterday?" asked Katie.

Father was silent.

"No one panic," he said finally.

Delthar shook his head, "This is a perfect time to panic. Cody, you and I were in that battle four hundred years ago. There is only one type of Dark Flame. And we destroyed them. Could they be back?"

Father turned to Delthar, "They would need a higher power for that."

"The Dark Prince could."

Father nodded sitting on a nearby stone seat, head in his hands.

"Should we send some men to nearby cities and towns?" asked the NightFang waiting for an order.

Father stood looking at the map on the stone.

"Bring Felix in here."

As the archer left, Katie turned to father.

"Shall Hailey and I go protect civilians?"

"Not a bad idea," said Delthar looking at Father.

Father shook his head, "I fear that bringing the WolfDragons would cause more harm to the people then it would help."

"But we must do something," Katie pleaded.

Father put a hand on her shoulder, "And we will, Princess."

That's when Felix entered the room. Father saluted him.

"Have you seen Edward?"

"No, not since yesterday."

"If he is not back in three minutes you must lead some NightFangs to Glenarm. You must protect the city."

"Me sir?"

"Yes, you must lead them. Join with Samuel and the NightBlades. Now go, assemble them."

"As you command."

As Felix left, Father turned to Delthar. A smile spread on his face.

"I have a plan. Katie, go make ready Hailey and the WolfDragons, this will include them."

When Katie left Father turned to the map on the table. He looked up at Delthar with a smile.

"We must gather the army and make for WinterFang Forest."

†††

Two hours later the army was assembled in different areas. Zander, along with Jack, and one hundred NightFangs and NightGuards around the outside of the house. Fifty NightGuards around the fortress. Father, Delthar, Mother, Ash, Alezandra, Heather and seven hundred Moon Soldiers gathered in the forest, west of the house. The army stretched left to right for several yards in each direction. One hundred NightFangs made the first two lines with two lines of two hundred and fifty NightWolves lined behind them. Two hundred and thirty NightBlades stood behind them while seventy NightHunters stayed back.

Each group of soldiers stood with their captains in the lead, except for Edward and Samuel. Katie and Hailey sat on their WolfDragons atop a small cliff, east of the house, east of the forest. Each soldier was in battle armor. Father turned to face the army. Some looked ready, others afraid.

"This is it! NightWolves, rise and defend! Let your swords be strong. NightFangs, the hour has come! Let your arrows be swift. NightGuards, stay strong! Let your swords be ready. NightHunters, do not be afraid! Let your Faith be strong. NightBlades, be ! Fight for the King. My children, fight to your last breath! Let not your hearts fail."courageous

He turned to Mother, "Winter Wolf, Anna,

my dear, be strong. We will win."

Mother smiled.

He turned again to the army, "Let this be an hour of faith and not fear! Stand with me! And fight! Today will be the sounds of battle. Tomorrow, victories song!"

The army stood tall, weapons ready, they were prepared to fight. Suddenly, Felix, and Samuel along with a few NightFangs and NightBlades came riding up to Father.

"Sir!" cried Felix.

Alezandra and several soldiers rushed to help as most of the Fangs were wounded. On the horses with the archers were several people from Glenarm. Many were coughing and bleeding.

"What happened?" asked Father.

Samuel dismounted his steed as did two female NightBlades behind him, "Dark Flames ambushed us. We were lucky to escape."

"Seventy men went to Glenarm...," said Delthar behind Father.

"And only seven returned," said Father finishing the sentence. "What of the rest of the civilians?"

Samuel shook his head in sadness, "The Flames are not far behind us, this is all the people we could bring back. I know not what has become of the city."

"Flames?" Mother inquired.

"Sara here says there must have been more than three thousand."

The NightBlade behind the captain, Sara,

stepped forward, "They were like shadows, we never saw them til it was too late."

Suddenly an arrow hit a NightFang in the back from a lone archer standing in the road, and he fell off his horse to the ground. Another NightFang in the front lines instantly struck the demon archer down with an arrow. Samuel along with Felix and the other Moon Soldiers joined in their respected ranks. Samuel stood in front of the row of Night-blades.

"Get these civilians to Alnor!" Delthar called out.

As the orders were carried out, Father stepped forward to see thousands of Dark Flames with swords drawn, marching towards them. No one moved, for they all stared at the bigger knight in the lead. Red eyes that flashed like fire, black armor as black as night, two hooked horns sticking out from the iron helmet. It was Cain! Father felt his heart skip a couple of beats at the sight of the demon. The chilling form of the demon caused ice like shivers up each soldier's spine. Cain kicked the dead Flame archer's body aside as he walked. Father was speechless and disgusted. Though she remembered what I said, Mother was in disbelief, I had been right about Cain.

"It's not possible," she said.

"No, it isn't," Father said to himself then turned to Mother. "Stay strong."

Mother had not seen those eyes in hundreds of years. Since she had been kidnapped, which led to the Great Battle.

Cain stopped seventy yards away, his army did the same. Father could hear the heavy breathing of the Black Knight. A demonic voice spoke in the language of the demons.

"Tira rith jakah (Hello old friends)."

His voice was deep and growly.

Father took a step towards him, "How are you alive?"

Cain laughed, "It's wonderful, isn't it?"

"Wolf killed you! You fell into a never ending hole," cried Mother.

"So he did. But now I have returned to claim my place in this world, to have my revenge. And I have a family member of yours to thank for my return."

"What do you mean?" Father roared.

"Never mind that, this world is mine."

"You will never have this world!" shouted Father drawing his sword.

"You will have to get through us first," said Delthar.

Cain laughed again, "Or you could surrender."

Father growled, "Never!"

Cain pointed his sword at Father, "So unwise."

He turned to his army and shouted, "Kill them!"

The demons charged. But Father stayed perfectly still. No one in the Army of the Moon moved. As the demons moved closer, Father turned to Ash.

"Sound the alarm."

Ash turned and shouted, "Now!"

A NightWolf sounded a horn and a few seconds later frost fire rained down from Riven and Rowen as they flew overhead. Dozens of Flames screamed in pain as the ice engulfed and impaled them.

"Ithai! (Fire!)" Father shouted keeping his focus on the army of darkness.

Dozens of NightFangs let arrows fly, each one finding a target. After the first line fired, they dropped to a knee letting the second line of Fangs fire, then they repeated several times. Father raised his sword in the air.

"For the King!"

The NightFangs stepped to the side, as Delthar and Samuel led the NightWolves and NightBlades, continuing to let fly the arrows. Ash transformed into a winged wolf and shot lightning from his mouth frying several Flames.

Alezandra transformed into the Sun Wolf, a wolf full of fire. She flapped her wings as several fire darts shot out into the ground in front of the Flames. As the demons ran over them they exploded sending each knight into the air.

Heather threw water ball after water ball, blasting several Flames. Mother put her hands together, and as she parted them, ice formed. She threw several balls of ice and snow at the demons. Father had sliced through several Flames, when he realized Cain had not moved.

The demon turned to him, they charged at one another. Both blades shot out from either side giving Father more advantage. But this was Cain, the Black Knight, Grandfather's archenemy.

In the air, Katie rode Riven as he blasted the demons with ice.

She yelled out to Hailey ahead of her, "Look out!"

Hailey looked up just in time to see a grey winged creature fly overhead. She ducked as it flew past. She turned back to see the creature circle back around.

"A gargoyle," she whispered.

Katie aimed an arrow and fired hitting the demon in the chest. It screamed as it fell to the ground.

"A scout!" she yelled.

Just then they both heard more shrieks as dozens of gargoyles charged from the sky. The girls stopped their WolfDragons next to each other.

"We got company," said Hailey watching the incoming attack.

"Cain has some new friends," Katie replied strapping another arrow. "I don't remember these from Grandfather's stories."

Hailey drew her sword.

"Let's fly!"

Both WolfDragons took into the sky breathing heavy ice. Gargoyles fell as Hailey slashed through each one they passed with her sword. Katie fired arrow after arrow, each one finding its mark.

Hailey looked to the ground at the main

battle, "Rowen, I have an idea."

Rowen flew lower towards a group of NightFangs as Hailey called out the order, "Archers, fire on the targets in the air!"

Dozens of arrows flew as gargoyles dropped from the sky. Those that survived scooped up Moon Soldiers and dropped them from the air.

Katie rode on Riven battling the demons. She looked to the ground to see many Moon Soldiers falling wounded. The Dark Flames had broken through the main line and attacked the NightFangs.

"I have to get down there," she told her WolfDragon.

"Want me to fly lower?"

"No, stay up here. Keep fighting."

"As you wish, Wolf Princess."

Katie then jumped from Riven's back. She landed on the ground near a NightFang who was bleeding from his leg.

"Are you alright?" she asked kneeling next to him.

"Other than my leg, I'm fine."

Katie gently put a hand on the deep cut. She closed her eyes speaking in Angelic, "Ith da nrame o da Kithak ana kalid (In the name of the King be healed)."

As she retreated her hand, the cut disappeared. The NightFang smiled.

"Thank you, daughter of Cody."

Rising to her feet she saw a NightWolf on the ground, an arrow protruding from his side. She knelt next to him seeing his eyes closed, hoping he was still alive. She took his right wrist, there was a pulse. She moved her hands down to the arrow. She saw blood running from the wound. She gently put a hand on the gash and arrow. She spoke softly in Angelic. As Katie opened her eyes the arrow fell from the skin as the hole stitched itself back together.

After a few seconds, the NightWolf breathed as his eyes opened.

"What the...?"

"You are healed now," said Katie with a smile.

The man looked around then at Katie, "Thank you, Princess Khil."

"Can you walk?"

"I believe so."

"Come, continue the fight."

Katie turned and immediately fired a golden arrow into a demon.

The demon army continued coming. Moon Soldiers went down quickly.

As Mother fought she turned to Heather, "River Wolf, water!"

Heather saw a group of Flames coming towards them, she instantly sprayed water to the ground. Mother blew frost like air freezing the water in place. As the Flames ran over it they immediately fell to the ground. In the air, Ash, in his wolf form, continued sending lightning down to the ground. Several Flames were reduced to ashes. Archers fired arrows at him. He swerved around them. One arrow hit his left wing making him stop. He turned to see Mother on the ground shoot frost on the Flames freezing them in place. She flew up to him as he turned into a human. She gently took the arrow from his arm, the wound was not deep. The arrow had struck perfectly between his armor.

"How are things up here?"

"I can send lightning all day. But it seems to amount to nothing. They keep coming."

Mother smiled, "Then why don't I join you?"

"How?"

"You are the Storm Wolf my son. I am the Winter Wolf."

Ash' face lit up with excitement, "A snow storm."

"Hmmm, a blizzard. The NightHunters can sneak around as the demons will not see in a storm of blowing snow."

They both put their swords together and closed their eyes. Lightning shot out from Ash' sword as snow swirled out of Mother's. Hailey saw this from Rowen's back.

She whispered to him, "Get me closer."

As Rowen flew overhead she jumped into the air next to Ash. She drew her sword and put it on the Storm Sword. Wind blew the snow ferociously. Soon the air was thick with a blowing blizzard. Just like Mother said, the demons could not see through the poor visibility, giving the Moon Soldiers plenty of targets. Silent and deadly the NightHunters sprung out from the shadows of the trees taking down the demonic army one by one, they were easy prey.

Felix stood with a band of NightFangs. With sword raised the archers drew arrows back. Quickly lowering his sword, arrows flew. Dark Flames went down one after another as each arrow found a mark.

It was then Delthar noticed several Flames running in the direction of Ahntharo Village.

"Wolves to me and follow!"

Dozens of NightWolves joined him. They arrived to see the Flames attacking the village of the Moon Soldiers. Many of the soldiers are married with kids. Delthar knew that was who the demons were going after.

He raised his sword with a shout, "Attack!"

As the Wolves fought, Alezandra appeared, blasting each demon with her fire while yelling in Angelic.

"Thyentan! Ith da foerc ta grosen rew! (Captain! Get the women and children away!)."

Delther knew what she meant and signaled his men to round up the people and get them away from the battle. Flames fell as Wolves cut through them.

The battle was going in the Army of the Moon's favor, when suddenly the snow was blasted back with waves of fire. Ash, Katie, Hailey, Mother and dozens of Moon Soldiers were blasted backwards to the ground and trees. The fire disappeared to reveal Cain holding his smoking hand towards them.

Thousands more Dark Flames charged from behind him. Father helped Mother to her feet. Suddenly Heather appeared between the two armies, water shooting from hand to hand. Cain stopped where he was. No one in the Army of the Moon moved. All waited to see what Heather would do.

"Go back thoo where you came!"

Cain laughed, "Young and foolish pup, you have nothing on me. What can you do against me, alone?"

Heather opened her hands as water sprayed out into the air.

She stared at the knight through the water, "Fear my wather, demon! I am the River Wolf. My King will deliver uth from your darkneth!"

With that, Heather burst her hands forward, water shot out towards the Black Knight. Father stood to his feet seeing Cain raise a hand at the oncoming water. Fire burst forth hitting the stream. Father noticed Heather tighten up as the water sprayed harder. A line of water pushing the line of fire as the flames fought back. Just as it seemed Heather would win Cain barked out in demonic as the fire suddenly burst through the stream into Heather blasting her backwards to the ground.

"Heather!" Katie screamed from Riven.

It was as if time had slowed down as Mother ran to Heather. Father rushed forth seeing the burnt marks on Heather's robe. She was knocked out. Father gently put a hand on her chest, put his ear to her heart, and heard the beat. She was alive, but badly wounded.

"Soldiers, get down here!"

Felix along with Matthias and a few NightBlades rushed down to him. Felix carefully scooped Heather into his arms and carried her away.

"Keep your eyes on her," Father told Matthias as he turned to face the demonic army.

Mother turned to Katie, "Help your sister!"

Katie flew to Heather's aid. Father turned to Mother.

"We must regroup."

"Yes. But we can't let them get to the house."

"How do we do that?" asked Ash landing next to them. "With Cain attacking like this, we would not survive. And now Heather is hurt."

Alezandra along with what Moon Soldiers were left gathered around them, weapons drawn. Father smiled as he looked into Mother's eyes.

"Then let's make sure they don't reach the house. We give it everything we got. For the King!"

Chapter 23
Help Arrives

We appeared in the house to find it empty. We checked every room, nothing.

"I have a bad feeling about this," said Edward.

Jenna walked about the Middle Room, "Where is everyone?"

"Invisible," I replied putting my backpack on a sofa in the Middle Room.

"Marcy and Nylanth?"

"We will have to hope they are alright."

That's when I heard distant clanking, like swords, "Outside!"

We came to the front door, opening it we found dozens of NightGuards standing still around the house. Two noticed and welcomed us.

"Where have you been?"

"What's going on?" I asked.

"Ez?"

I turned to Captain Zander coming towards us as he removed his Wolfhelm.

"Captain. Good to see you."

"Where have you three been?"

"Long story," replied Edward. "Do you know what is going on?"

"What are those people doing here?" asked Jenna looking to the civilians of Glenarm being helped by soldiers.

"They are from Glenarm, the city was apparently destroyed."

"Destroyed?" I asked. "What do you mean?"

"The battle has begun, Katie is on her WolfDragon, Cody, your father, led an army of Wolves, Fangs, Hunters and Blades to the forest. We are here to protect the house."

Battle?! That's when I heard the sound again, the echo of swords clanking. Cain must have unfroze time. The fight had already started.

"Follow us," I motioned to Zander.

"Cody ordered us to stay here."

Realizing Zander did not know it was Cain attacking, I turned back to him, "Father needs more help than Alnor does."

"Are you sure about this, Moon Wolf?"

Before I could answer, a NightGuard cried out, "Incoming!"

A boulder landed near us shaking the ground. We dove away from it.

"Where did that come from?!" Jenna cried standing to her feet.

"The forest?" I wondered.

"Only one answer," said Edward next to me. "Catapults."

Then it hit me, they were trying to destroy the house. Another boulder flew out of the trees toward us.

"No!" I screamed.

But to my relief the giant rock hit something before it reached the house and fell to the ground. My heart leaped for joy, Father had put up Alnor Wik's force shield. It surrounded the house on all sides.

Jenna stood to her feet as another boulder flew over the house, missing the shield, "The shield won't stay up long with boulders like that."

Glancing towards WinterFang I shouted, "To the battle!"

Zander turned to his men and motioned for them to follow while a few stayed behind. We dashed for the trees to see the sight. Hundreds if not thousands of Flames were everywhere in battle with only hundreds of Moon Soldiers.

"Heather!"

I turned towards Jenna noticing Heather on the ground surrounded by soldiers. My heart sank, she was hurt. I rushed to her side to see the blood on her side and the burn marks on her robe. I looked up at Katie who sat on the other side of our sister.

"Is she...?"

"Alive, barely, I am healing her as best I can."

I felt a tear roll down my face as I gazed at my sister's still face, the crimson color ran from her side turning the snow red, "This is my fault, if only I had gotten here sooner."

I felt a hand on my shoulder, "You don't know that. No one knows what could have happened."

I looked to Edward who smiled. Suddenly a bright blue and green flash erupted between two trees as Marcy and Nylanth emerged into the forest. They made it!

"Marcy!" I shouted through thought.

Marcy happily nuzzled me. Nylanth jumped on Edward with delight. Several Moon Soldiers ran at him but Edward was quick to defend.

"He is friend."

"Where did he come from?" asked a NightHunter.

"Long story."

"The same place as Marcy here," I replied.

I turned to my mouse friend, "What happened to you two?"

"We went through the portal in your uncle's land, only to arrive back in his land in a different area. We had to wait several hours before we found a new portal."

I laughed and hugged her, "Will you help us fight now?"

Marcy turned to the battle in motion.

"This is your land?"

I nodded, "My home."

"Just point us in the direction of the enemy," said Nylanth coming up to me followed by Edward. "We will follow you."

I gazed up to see Ash in the sky send a bolt

of lightning to the ground reducing several Flames and gargoyles to ashes. But more Flames still came. The NightGuards instantly attacked.

With sword raised, I turned to Edward and my sister, "Go!"

Edward at once let an arrow fly into a demon as Jenna went to help Alezandra. Marcy whipped her long tail around hitting several Flames. Nylanth with his claws began shredding several gargoyles in the air to pieces.

Zander came to my side, "Is that Cain?"

I took a deep breath as my eyes locked onto the huge knight.

"Yes, it is."

I noticed Father in battle with Cain. The Black Knight flipped him to his back and raised his sword above his chest. The memory of the dream of Father dying entered my mind. I would not let this happen. I took a deep breath as I walked towards him.

"Cain!"

Cain glanced up at me and growled.

"Moon Wolf, it is a pleasure to meet you in person at last."

That voice made my insides shiver. Cain took a step towards me.

"So, you survived?"

He continued towards me, leaving Father on the ground. My heart sank again, he knew we had been gone.

I growled, "It takes more than that to get rid of me. I am the Moon Wolf, and I will run no longer."

Cain raised his sword above his head.

"Then let me show you how it is done!"

† † †

(This section told to me by Edward)

Edward fired arrow after arrow at Flames and gargoyles. He saw Nylanth fly in the sky picking up demons then dropping them. A gargoyle flew down onto Edward snarling at him. He fell to the ground with the creature on him trying to bite his neck, his bow next to him. Using his hands to keep the teeth away he kicked the demon in the chest knocking it to the ground. Rolling over he grabbed the bow strung an arrow and fired it into the gargoyles head, it plopped to the ground dead. Edward scrambled to his feet withdrew the arrow and fired it into an oncoming knight. Suddenly he was hit in the head knocking him to the ground. He rolled over to see a knight lift a huge sword above his chest. At that moment the knight fell to the ground his head rolling away as Nylanth jumped onto the body. Edward rose up again scratching the Draat's head.

"Thank you my friend."

"I fight with you."

Suddenly Nylanth's eyes grew wide and his body shook. Edward saw it, the arrow in the Draat's side. Beyond him was a knight stringing another. The Nightfang was quicker and felled the demon with his own arrow. Nylanth fell to the ground as Edward knelt next to him scrambling for the arrow in his fur.

"Nylanth stay calm, I will help you."

He felt claws on his arm as the Draat gently took hold of his arm.

"I...give my life."

A tear formed rolling down Edward's cheek. Nylanth smiled.

"You freed me, and now I saved your life."

"Nylanth, please..."

"Fight...on."

The Draat's eyes closed. Edward felt his heart drop like a rock. Nylanth was gone. The archer slowly rose from the ground gazing around him. The demon army was too big. But not if he could help it. At once he strung three arrows on his bow firing all in one shot, each one finding a demon.

†††

Cain swung his giant black blade towards my head. I ducked and swiped at his legs. He jumped and brought his blade down to mine. But as our swords met the impact knocked me backward to the ground. I struggled to stand, looking up to see the great knight swing again. I barely blocked and was sent to the ground again. I rose to my knees and felt the necklace around my neck. My breath was like smoke as I was breathing hard. My eyes hurt from the harsh wind. I grabbed hold of the cross and closed my eyes.

"This is for Emmanuel. I am a wolf, no surrender, no retreat."

I swung my sword with all my strength at the knight's neck.

"I'm no longer afraid of you! I will not run!"

"Fear is all you have left girl!"

He held up a hand and I was blasted backward by an invisible force. I landed in the snow, my leg would not move. Cain walked slowly toward me sword pointed at my neck.

I stayed still on my back ready for the pain...

A sudden voice interrupted Cain's sure victory.

"Cain!"

The voice seemed to break through the sound of the battle as my family and army stopped where they were, even the Flames halted, looking in the direction of the voice. Cain looked up from his position. I tilted my head backward enough to see an archer dressed in white, an arrow was poised at the knight. I could not focus on who it was, for there was a white hood on the archer's head. It was a white color unlike any I had seen, this was no NightFang. But that voice, that voice was familiar. It spoke again.

"Let her go."

That's when it clicked, not he, it was a she! Aunt Hannah! I heard Cain laughing.

"And who is going to stop me, you? You are

alone, foolish to come against me."

I looked back at Hannah who had a big smile on her face.

"I'm not alone."

A howl burst forth from the trees. I heard footsteps, seeming to come from behind my aunt. They were getting closer, as part wolf I could tell they were running.

I looked at Cain who was on his feet, still as a statue, staring in the direction of the howl. As I watched, from within the trees a man dressed in black ran passed the archer towards Cain, gold sword raised.

As I focused on the man, I saw the green eyes. I felt my heart leap. Grandfather! Suddenly, from the trees, more figures appeared. I turned over on my stomach and saw Grandmother, the White Wolf, followed by several of my aunts and cousins and my brother's best friend Cedric, in his bear form.

The new army charged full speed through the smoke into the Flames. The Moon Soldiers rejoined the battle. I turned to Cain who was raising his sword above my neck.

At that moment, a great black wolf leaped over me knocking him to the smoking ground. The wolf landed on the dirt and spinning around transformed into Grandfather. Sword raised, he charged at the knight. Cain leapt to his feet and their swords touched. Edward appeared helping me to my feet. We both ran to the trees watching the great duel unfold. I glanced around, looking at the new arrivals.

"How did they know to come here?" I asked Edward.

He smiled, "Your grandfather must have sensed Cain."

Just then a massive animal leapt over us into a group of Dark Flames, it was a cross between a lion and a tiger. My cousin Laylin in tan liger form. After taking out several demons the liger transformed into Laylin's human form with long brown hair. She winked at me then joined her twin sister Raylin in further fighting. A bright blue light shined knocking several demons back. The light faded revealing NightLight, another cousin, in her black and blue wolf form.

As I listened, I heard her say, "I am here. Now you will all die."

She quickly blasted a few Flames with blue light from her mouth.

I laughed. She transformed into a girl with long black hair dressed in black and blue robes, opening her hands as a blue sword appeared on them. She then let out a howl as four wolves came rushing from the forest to her aid.

"Ashlynn, Tobias, Salty, Geana, attack!"

The wolves rushed into battle taking out each Flame they touched. Another boulder landed near my cousin, so NightLight closed her eyes and lifting her hands with vines from the ground, pushed her hands forth as the vines shot out towards the catapults. The vines wrapped around them crushing them to the ground.

"You can't beat us little girl."

I gulped at the sound of those words, little girl, I knew what was coming. I turned to see my aunt Kaitlin instantly slice off the heads of five Flames with one swing of her fire sword. Never, ever, call my aunt little.

I turned to Grandmother as she fought what looked like thirty Flames, alone. I thought to help, but Edward pulled me back. As we watched, Grandmother put a hand on the ground, suddenly all the Flames were blasted backwards to the ground. She, the White Wolf, was powerful. Turning to the sky I saw Ash and my mom send a furious blizzard to the ground encasing several Flames in blocks of ice. With one twirl of his sword Ash sent dozens of lightning bolts to the ground, frying all of them.

Edward nudged me nodding his head to my right. I saw it, Nylanth, dead. My heart grieved.

"I'm so sorry NightFang."

"This battle is won," he replied with a smile.

I smiled, yes it was. A line of frost fire from Riven and Rowen encased several Flames in ice as they soared through the air. Katie had rejoined the battle, I waved at my sister as she turned to me from her WolfDragon. It was at that moment, I felt a strength come over me, such as I had never felt.

I looked back towards the duel between Grandfather and Cain. It seemed to be enhancing, becoming more intense. Cain opened his hands as fire appeared. He threw fireball after fireball as Grandfather jumped dodging each one of them. He landed on his feet pointing his sword at Cain as a gold light shot out from the blade. The light blasted Cain in his chest sending him into a tree. Grandfather lowered his sword breathing heavily.

"So, you're alive. Four hundred years ago you fell into that pit."

Cain laughed as he stood to his feet.

"You thought you could get rid of me? I waited for hundreds of years in that hole to regain my strength. But now I have returned and I will have my revenge!"

Father came up behind me, his eyes fixed on Grandfather as he turned to me.

"So, you were right about The Dark Flames."

I shook my head, "This battle is won."

Father turned about to see the Army of the Moon and Grandfather's army finishing off the last of the demons. He turned to me with a smile. Suddenly a vision appeared. Opening my eyes I turned to my father who was kneeling next to me, I was trembling.

"What was it?" he asked.

"You...must get to Ahntharo Village, it...its Delthar."

Father was gone in an instant. Jenna bounded up to us in her wolf form with a smile. I turned to see Cain charge at Grandfather.

"Prepare to die, Wolf!"

But at the last possible second Grandfather held up his right hand. A rush of wind let out from his palm pushing Cain back. He struggled to walk any closer to Wolf, but he was not about to surrender. He continued pushing against the wind. Grandfather raised his left hand to double the force. Cain struggled more to stand his ground. His feet were slipping from under him. He pushed harder.

"Go back to whence you came!" Grandfather shouted.

Cain got on all fours and began crawling towards him with all his strength.

"In the name of the King, go back to whence you came!"

That did it, Cain flew backwards into the air to the ground several yards away. He slowly stood to his feet, though I could tell he was weakened. He pointed his sword at Grandfather.

"I do not answer to you."

Grandfather pulled out his sword and began making a circle in the air between him and Cain. I saw Cain step back as a smile spread on my face. Grandfather's energy orb was forming. Electric currents spread throughout the circle which had turned dark purple. I saw Grandfather smile.

"You will answer to the King!" he roared.

With a swipe of his sword, the orb of energy shot towards Cain with such force, no one could outrun it, even though the Black Knight tried. Cain roared as the orb engulfed him.

"From the grave darkness rises, and to the grave it returns," said Edward behind me. "Never to darken the world again."

"When light breaks the dark, evil shall be gone with the arrival of dawn," I replied with a smile.

At the same moment, the sun peeked through the clouds shining on the duel.

"Dawn," I said quietly.

A few seconds later the orb along with Cain exploded into a brilliant shower of bright sparks. We shielded our eyes from the exploding light. When the light faded, Grandfather turned to us.

With a smile on his face and sword raised in the air he said, "It is finished."

We all raised our swords high and cheered. I embraced my brother and sisters in celebration. I felt a hand on my shoulder. Turning to see Edward. He kissed my cheek as I threw my arms around him. The battle was over. As I hugged my mom, Grandfather came up to me holding Ethril.

"Thank you for finding the clues to Cain."

I was stunned, "You knew?"

"You had a vision, you solved the puzzle."

I was confused how he knew of my dream, but I decided this was not the time to ask questions, "You're welcome."

Grandfather put a gentle hand on my shoulder, "I have always told you I would help you."

I saw my father hugging Hannah. Two siblings and best friends, together. As they let go, Hannah turned to me with a smile. I leapt into her arms hugging her tight.

"Thank you, for saving my life," I said.

"You're welcome."

"Ezeryah!"

Turning I saw Hailey running towards me, "Sister, what is it?"

The two armies had stopped at the sound of my worried voice.

Hailey took a deep breath, "It... It is Heather."

"What is it?" asked Marcy.

I gulped, "My sister."

I was gone in an instant, to my sister, who was wounded. I could not bear the thought of what I would find. Arriving where Heather had been with Katie kneeling over her, I felt fear again. Riven rested on a boulder behind them.

"Katie, is she... ?"

Jenna appeared next to me as did Father. Katie stood up to face us. I saw it, Heather was nowhere to be seen. My greatest fear had come true, Heather was gone, the tears came. But then seeing Katie point behind me, a smile spread on her face. Confused, I turned, there, standing and smiling... Heather! Rushing to her I threw my arms around my sister.

I heard Father call out, "Heather lives!"

Gazing at my sister, I could not help but wonder... how? A thought entered, Katie, the Lady of Healing. Heather laughed as she held me close. Hugging her back, I thanked Emmanuel. My sister lived. Jenna joined in as did the rest of my siblings. Mother let out a howl as did many of us, the battle was over.

Sadly, Delthar had been slain protecting the children of Ahntharo Village. Now, five captains remained, Father, Edward, Zander, Matthias and Samuel. Even though we lost many soldiers, many more lived, victory.

† † †

Later that night, we rejoiced with music and dance. Marcy sat on the ground in front of me while I sat on a log watching the celebration around a great bonfire. I laughed as Marcy attempted to dance with the music.

The NightFang Captain sat down next to me saying, "You know, you should write a book about this adventure."

I loved how his mind worked, "A grand idea."

As the celebration continued, I could not help but wonder something.

"Edward, how did you come back? You were surrounded."

Edward smiled, "Simple, after defeating our attackers, I waited until 2021. During those sixteen years, I travelled the world. Fought demons where I could. Then came to meet you and Jenna on the mountain. I also had a little help after you and Jenna left."

He nodded towards a banquet table where

Grandfather talked with Kaitlin. When he saw us, he smiled. I looked back at Grandfather who saluted me.

As I saluted him a thought did linger, "Edward, while you were in the past, did you tell Grandfather of Cain's returning?"

"Indeed not," the NightFang replied. "I know not how your Grandfather knew. It is curious, someone must have told the Alpha of the danger, but, who?"

Several NightWolves and NightFangs played instruments, led by Zander on the fiddle, as Heather, Alezandra and others tap danced. NightHunters and NightBlades danced while twirling their daggers in the air.

The roaring bonfire, with help from Alezandra in her wolf form, lit up the starry sky as the flames grew higher. Mother had created an ice rink near the house which several soldiers skated.

Jenna sat next to me and Edward on my left. My sister shuffled her watch around in her hands. She smiled at me as I smiled back.

Every so often someone would come to the three of us asking for the tale of our adventures through time. I looked up to see Katie and Hailey flying on Riven and Rowen around the sky.

I felt a tap on my left shoulder and turned to Edward who held a handout to me. Smiling, I took it as he lifted me to my feet. As we danced, I saw Father dancing with Mother. Grandfather and Grandmother as well as many Moon Soldiers joined in.

We did it, the battle was over. Cain and his Flames were finally gone. No more nightmares. With my family, my Father's army, and Grandfather's army around me, I felt peace. It was the first time in a longtime. It felt amazing.

† † †

Later, as the celebration continued, I walked alone to The Glade of WinterFang Forest. When I arrived I went to the middle of the stone pillars, kneeling in the snow. I crossed my right arm over my heart and prayed quietly.

"Thank you, Emmanuel."

As I opened my eyes, I thought there was a glimpse of a knight in white armor standing by a tree. The Knight saluted me, I saluted Him back, then, He vanished. Feeling the Spirit come over me, I felt calm. After a while I returned to rejoin the armies to celebrate.

Chapter 24
A Time of Peace

A week later I sat on my bed staring into space, Marcy slept quietly on the floor. A knock came to my door.

"Come in."

My father entered holding a present.

"Happy Voldar's Reeth."

I smiled, "You as well."

"Open it," he said handing me the grey colored paper that housed my gift.

I opened it to find a beautiful silver crescent moon necklace. Nine tiny diamonds lay within one side of the moon.

"Dad, it is beautiful!"

He hooked it around my neck with a smile, "You're welcome. But I have one more gift."

"Really?"

I felt my heart beat faster, I could not guess what it was.

Father took a deep breath, "Well, no one can replace Delthar. He was a great friend. But there is one who could take his place as Night-

Wolf Captain."

My eyes grew, "Father, are you saying...?"

"Yes, I would love for you to become the new NightWolf Captain. Your courage, determination, leadership, and faith, are the qualities of a captain. If you want to, I'm not saying you have to."

I was not sure what to think, me a captain? I never thought of it. I could be in charge of the entire NightWolf force.

"Father, this is amazing, thank you for thinking of me for this position. And, yes, I accept."

We both smiled and laughed.

"Captain Ezeryah has arrived," Father replied.

I held the necklace in my fingers, it was beautiful.

"So after this last week, how are you?"

I looked up at him, "Tired."

Father smiled.

"It has been a long two weeks for everyone." He sat next to me, "We are almost ready to open presents."

I looked at the floor, "Father, are you mad at me?"

He turned to me.

"For leaving? For going to find the truth of Cain's return? No, if I had been in your shoes, I would have done the same thing."

I kept my eyes down.

"I did not want to tell you about my dream."

"Because of Kelly?"

I was stunned, how did he know that?

"Yes."

I heard him take a deep breath.

"Writing?"

I looked up as he eyed my notebook on my dresser.

"This passed adventure."

Father flipped through the pages, there were only a few.

"You know, when my sister died, I had no idea what to do. I felt my world being torn in two. Turns out it was the push we needed to fight the Great Battle."

I took a deep breath, "She sounded beautiful."

Father smiled looking at the notebook.

"Any idea what this one will be called?"

I thought long and hard about that. I had not come up with a good title yet. Then it came.

"Return of the Black Knight."

Father smiled, "I like it, it fits."

"Even after this adventure, I still long for something more."

Father sat beside me as he handed me my notebook.

"Katie has expressed a desire to write a book."

"Really?"

"Of when she and Hailey found the Wolf-Dragons."

The thought of the WolfDragon's story being written excited me. My heart pounded with delight. But then I remembered...

"Didn't you write a book, Father?"

Father smiled, "I wrote two."

"Two?"

"Oh yes, of when I came to Ireland the first time. Then an adventure with Hannah and I."

"She is your best friend."

"And younger sister."

"I would love to read them."

"Perhaps tonight, I shall read to you all."

"I would love that. Everyone should write a book."

"Many of your aunts and uncles already did. I will have to talk to them about publishing."

I heard Father take a deep breath as he stared at the sky outside my window.

"Ez, you remember? I told you that I feared peace would never come in this world."

"I remember well."

"I was afraid. I'd forgotten what faith was. But you turned it around, you made me realize what I had missed."

"Missed what?"

"That faith is stronger than fear. Snow falls at this moment, I feel the same peace you did."

I laid my head in his arms as he hugged me tight.

"My brother Rudolph has really been a king all these years?"

I giggled, "The castle was amazing dad. He, now has the power of ice and snow. Married to Queen Anara."

Father smiled, "That was a treat for you to see him."

I laughed, "He was more than a little surprised to see us too."

Father laughed with me.

"I can imagine so. It does make sense why I have not heard from him in so long."

It was then I remembered, the package Uncle Rudolph had sent back with me. Father stood to his feet as I dug under my bed and gently pulled out the leather wrapped item.

"Uncle gave this to me before we left."

"What is it?"

"All he said was, his life."

Father opened the leather to reveal a book. The brown leather covered parchment type paper perfectly intact. On the cover were written these words in gold.

Legend of the Winter King

"What do we have here?"

I moved my hand over the soft leather cover.

"Could it be the story of what happened to him?"

Father moved his hand to open it, but drew back.

"It is not right to open such a book here, not yet. We must share this with the world. Let everyone know what happened to Rudolph. Your Grandfather would want to know."

He rewrapped the leather carefully around the book and handed it to me.

"Keep it safe, the time will come to reveal it."

"With my life, Father."

I placed the book back under my bed then sat down on the covers.

Father sat next to me staring at the notebook, "You know, I was thinking. Why not talk to your grandfather? I'm sure he has plenty of stories to tell."

"He has told me many."

"True, but they are stories you could write about."

I smiled, why had I not thought of that? The one man that had had enough adventures in his life to fill a six thousand page book was the ticket. To write a book about him, would be an adventure in itself.

Father wrapped his arms around me.

"You are one of the bravest warriors I have ever known. I am so proud of you, Moon Wolf."

"Thanks dad. Where is Grandfather Wolf?"

"I believe he is in the fortress. But first, it is the first day of Voldar's Reeth, time for presents. Everyone has assembled."

That, I was certainly ready for.

Chapter 25

I Know What to Call the Books

A few hours later I went to Grandfather as he sat in the White Fortress, meditating.

As I neared him, I heard, "Come, sit by me."

Even with his eyes closed he knew I was there.

He spoke as I sat next to him, "You know, four hundred years ago, The Great Battle was fought and won. Lieutenant Python had asked me, 'Is there a chance Cain could ever return?' I told him no, because I did not believe it could happen."

I put a hand on his shoulder, "You had no way of knowing."

"Until you had a dream."

I smiled, "I was told you had stories. For I need an idea to write."

Grandfather smiled and opened his green eyes, "Plenty. I have many stories I could tell you. Many stories about I, Commander Wolf. Good, bad, fun, adventurous stories. I can tell you of the Battle of Zion."

"The Battle of Zion?"

"The battle that started it all. The reason we fight even today. The reason I was sent to earth."

Closing my eyes, I felt the Spirit of the King come over me, "For the first time in a long time, I feel happy."

"As you should, there is much to be glad of this day."

I turned to Grandfather, "How did you defeat Cain? I mean, from all the stories, he was stronger then you."

Grandfather turned to me, "Cain was in that hole for hundreds of years. During the Great Battle, Cain lost all of his powers." He turned and drew Ethril, "And this is why."

Grandfather pointed to five words on the gold blade.

I read them aloud carefully, "The Sword of the Wolf."

"When two archenemies meet in battle, only one can be victorious'. Only one weapon could defeat Cain, and this is it. During the Great Battle, I ran Cain through with the blade, thus dispelling his powers."

"So you living while Cain was dead, you continued gaining powers."

"Exactly. I became stronger than him."

It all became clear to me at that very second. Grandfather was the most powerful being in the world at that very moment.

"But, remember this, I do not believe Cain was ever dead. Only his power. NightLight will have to tell you of that."

"Why my cousin?"

"She may know of why Cain came back. She was the one who told me of your vision."

I was bewildered, "How did she know?"

"She will tell you when she is ready. You may want to write a book about it."

Closing my eyes comprehending what I had just heard. A thought entered my mind.

"Do you think he regained all of his strength?"

"Cain, no. He is powerful yes, but I do not believe the Black Knight was like he had been four centuries ago."

"But he had enough power to survive the hole, to return."

Grandfather looked at me in concern.

"I do not believe it was all from Cain."

"You mean the...?"

"Yes."

I closed my eyes in deep thought.

"Why me?"

"What do you mean?"

"Why was I the one that had the dream? I mean anyone could have had a dream like that."

I heard Grandfather take a deep breath.

"I believe it was because you are the Moon Wolf, Lady of visions."

That made perfect sense.

"I was afraid of Cain because he put these dreams in my mind."

Grandfather turned to me, "No, it was not Cain."

"What?"

"I believe it was Elohim's Son who gave you those dreams."

I went into deep thought about that. If Emmanuel was the reason for the visions of Cain, then that meant only one thing, "It was a warning," I replied.

"Exactly, Emmanuel knows that you have the power of visions. So He gave you those dreams, because He knew you were the only one who could figure out what they meant. And you did, for everyone. You figured out the clues, you made the discovery. You saved a lot of lives last week."

"Not everyone."

"Glenarm will be rebuilt, Ez. But you saved the entire world from Cain's wrath."

"Cain's plan still worked though. He sent me on a wild goose chase so he could attack the future. I felt like I had failed."

"You did no such thing, why? Because you still found the answers."

I nodded, "I had help finding the clues."

Grandfather turned to me, "I am so proud of you, Ezeryah. And I am so humbled to be your Grandfather. You are an incredible warrior."

"Thank you."

"You are a hero. And will always be remembered as one."

I smiled at the thought, it was a moment as if everything had just become clear in life. I was the hero who saved not only my family, but the entire world as well.

"Faith really does win battles."

"Fear will not win wars, only Faith in Elohim."

"Grandfather, would you mind if I wrote a book, of your life?"

"Ez, I would be honored."

I went into deep thought. Then the idea I had desired for so long, finally sparked, "I think I know what I shall call the books. For I feel there will be more than one."

"What's that?"

I smiled, "Wolf Legacy."

Epilogue

I, Ezeryah, write this book to you as a way for you to know the things which have happened. There are still battles being fought everyday against the demons, but I will not forget this adventure. Continue the journey with me as I write more. Grandfather will be here soon to begin on the first book of Wolf Legacy. I could not be more excited. As for you, continue fighting your own battles, Elohim and Emmanuel are with you. And remember... faith is stronger than fear!

About the Author

E.J. Sobetski is a Christian author with a love for wolves, dragons, knights, castles and big battles. He has 25 books planned altogether.

He achieved a red belt in Tae Kwon Do & sang in homeschool choir for 7 years. He currently teaches Jr. High and High School kids at his church and is a guest speaker at his Church youth camp every summer.

He is the youngest of 7 and uncle of 17. EJ resides in Eastern Nebraska.

www.ingramcontent.com/pod-product-compliance
Lightning Source LLC
Chambersburg PA
CBHW030858060726
47591CB00005B/1331